ALTERED

SELVES

CHRISTOPHER HAWKE

Dedicated to those who fight for the integrity of their souls.

CONTENTS

ACKNOWLEDGMENTS

Thanks to my family for the years of love and understanding—for believing in me even when it seemed to defy reason. Thanks to the many editors who worked on this novel. I couldn't have written *Altered Selves* without you. Mary Ann Kersten, Caryn Gross-Devincenti, and Traci Hall you are fabulous women with hearts of gold!

Man is at the bottom an animal, midway, a citizen, and at the top, divine. But the climate of this world is such that few ripen at the top.

—Henry Ward Beecher

~ ONE ~

ANDREW I

Tremol and Arrot's combined fat pins me to the pebble-strewn floor of my cell. My arms and legs are sticks and weak as the bones in them. I thrash, hoping to hit them, but my diet has made me weak. They strip me and do as they wish—as they have always done. It is over as quickly as childhood.

After, the brothers clang a plate of moldy bread and a cup of water onto the floor and leave with a click of the lock. Their rotten-onion stench lingers.

I tear off bits of bread and crawl to the sackcloth in the corner where my injured dove waits. "You're almost ready to fly again."

Her wings flap with acceptance. They'd crush her if they'd heard her coo.

Distant holiday memories leave me with the vague feeling I once belonged somewhere, though the torturous monotony of endless days have become far more real. I grip the frozen iron bars between the stone walls and peer out the window at freedom. Below, beyond the first row of trees, ashen fog takes over. More than anything, I want to be in that forest, running from this stone fortress, toward a place where a warm family laughs among the shimmering, colored lights of Christmas. What little I remember about who I am resides in those memories. I wish I could fit between the bars and fly away, as I hope my friend will. Hope of her escape is somehow enough to wake in the morning.

Frigid air moans. I huddle in what's left of my rotted sheet, cover my stick legs, and try to forget my burning cough. I dream of making the sheet into a noose.

The sun is high in the sky, but the cold pricks at my skin. The window delights me to something new. She stands at the wooden gate on the edge of the forest, as though floating on air. Her dress is like white flowers on pale, bare skin. Blond hair showers her shoulders and the curve of her waist. I can't see from such a distance, but I imagine her face as lovely as freedom.

She raps on the outer castle gate and waits, standing on her toes to peer over. I beg God they don't see her. I want to call a warning, but can't find my voice.

Arrot ambles near the gate holding his sword close to his great, lumpy body, his ribbons of fat concealed by a brown woolen robe.

My knuckles turn white on the window's bars. "Run. Run." But, the words don't reach her, they barely leave my mouth.

Arrot heaves the gate open.

She's gone, vanished into the fog.

My captors throw a new cellmate to the floor and crash the door shut. His tattered clothes and bleached leather skin sags on his bony frame. He smells as if exhumed from a grave.

"Now you've got a *friend*," taunts Tremol through his boil-ridden lips.

The downed man's ribcage pulses into a muffled laugh. His pepper-gray storm of a head turns, exposing a pecked-out eye. He spits from the sides of his mouth with a strained chuckle. "Kill ol' Sedgwick they say. Lock him up. But I'm right here, doing my job."

My insides churn at the sight of my sad company.

His tongue flits about the rim of his mouth. He swings his arms in an effort to flip onto his back. "You Andrew Blight?"

"I don't know," I admit.

"I'm sure of it." He turns over and sighs. "Nights are longer when you don't know who you are. I remember that."

"Who are you?"

"Your redeemer." Sedgwick laughs.

I've been alone so long I even welcome the company of this corpse. What judgment could I bring when I don't know my own name? "Where did they find you?"

"They didn't find me," he groans. "I found them."

"You wanted to be captured?"

"To get here." He sits up and leans against the stone wall.

"I don't understand." My mind searches for a glimmer of my own importance. "Where did you come from?"

A smile creases his face. "Same place as you."

"Where did I come from?" I look to the corner at the sound of a squawk. My dove's gone. I leap on Sedgwick and squeeze his bony neck with all my might. "What did you do with her?"

He frees himself with a jerk of his head and arms. "You don't have the strength."

Sedgwick uncups his hands to reveal the bird. He tosses the dove heavenward and she finds freedom, flying out the prison window. I hold a prayer in my heart as she fights air until safely in the forest.

My cellmate breaks into a phlegmy chuckle and struggles to stand. "No one here ever really knows where they come from. The question is, can you bear what I have to tell you?"

A cloud lifts and light courses through the barred window revealing the cell's filth. My only friend has flown away.

Sedgwick rubs his neck. "You've just started to believe you have a soul. You have seen her haven't you?"

I swallow a mouthful of spit. "I saw a woman. You couldn't have seen."

His mouth turns down. "Do you think you have the slightest clue what's real in this place?"

Not only is the universe stranger than we imagine, it is stranger than we can imagine.

—J. B. S. Haldane, *Possible Worlds and Other Papers*, 1927

~ TWO ~

JAMES I

The office bustled with typing, phone calls, and ass-kissing chatter.

A red-haired, big-boned man leaned over my desk. "Is she cracking the whip? Don't worry, she does it to everyone."

His necktie strangled until his cheeks were rosy. He offered me his hand. "Mike Sanders."

An overgrown child, I thought. The kind of guy who leaves a fraternity for a sales job, marries his college girlfriend, and cuts off his balls so he fattens up like a steer.

He leaned in close and shook my hand. "So, what are you doing for Sterling?"

I pointed at the sign on my desk. "Advertising Specialist."

"Specialist! Man, I didn't even know—"

The phone buzzed.

I held a finger in the air and reached for the receiver. "Maxi?"

Mike trotted off toward the lunch room, waving as he passed a row of cubicles.

† † †

Maxine Sterling sat on a couch in her office huddled over a stack of cardboard-backed mockups. She wore a muted gold disco-era top and black nylon slacks. A tuft of hair plumed from her head—the feathers of a great brunette Cockatoo.

She waved me over, excited. "Shut the door."

"Is that new?" I asked.

"What? This?" She patted her mating-call bob. "Do you like it?"

"Very fashionable." I sat beside her and scanned through the stack, making sure to pause thoughtfully at each picture. They sucked.

She was giddy, rubbing her hips against the suede cushion in apparent anticipation. "Dirk came up with these. He gave them to me an hour ago."

I bet he did, I thought. Don't blow it. You're still in the angel phase. You've got at least another month before everyone realizes your shit stinks. A month after that, you'll be lucky if they sit next to you in the cafeteria.

I checked her placenta-powdered cheek-line for signs of distrust, and spread the ads on the table. "Brilliant. Which do you like most?"

Her eyeliner stretched with a squint. "None of them. They're shit."

My hand paused over the next ad. "What do you mean?"

"It scares me that you think these are good."

"I don't understand."

She clicked her pumps back to the suede leather throne behind her desk. "I only showed you these to see if you could be trusted. There are two kinds of people: 'yes' men and straight shooters. Now I know which you are."

I picked up a picture of a tiara-crowned poodle that looked to be wearing an Angeri original. "Don't you think this is daring?"

"What the hell is daring about a goddamn dog in a nightgown?"

I bent my notepad to the point of breaking. "Doesn't it reach the bestiality demographic?"

She checked my face, but I didn't give her the satisfaction of a smile.

"Get out."

✝ ✝ ✝

Mike Sanders held a plastic mug under a running faucet in the lunchroom. "You said that? I should have warned you. She finds ways to 'test' people."

"Has she tested you?"

Mike turned off the water and smiled. "She hit on me at last year's New Year's Eve party. She was sloshed."

If she was hitting on Mike, I doubted she could still walk.

"She asked if I wanted to go home with her. I told her I couldn't, and she threw a wine spritzer in my face."

"Really? What did you do?"

He shrugged. "What could I do? I left."

At some point, I'd lost track of my one-night stands. "You could have taken her in the other room," I said under my breath. "Instant promotion."

"Or firing," Mike said.

A black man in a navy-blue, pinstripe suit strolled in and grabbed his lunch out of the fridge.

Mike raised his voice. "On Monday she told me the entire thing had been a *test*."

The black man slid a frozen lunch into the microwave. "That woman lies like Lucifer's ugly twin sister."

Mike Sanders pointed to me. "Rudy, this is James, the new guy. He's going to save the world."

"I don't know about that," I said. "I'm the new ad guy."

Rudy shook my hand. "Welcome aboard . . . the S.S. Bullshit."

Heartwarming. "Thanks."

"Rudy's in sales," offered Mike. "They just laid off half his team."

I tried to look as though I cared. "Bummer."

Rudy popped open the microwave door. "You'd do well to steer clear of The Pad."

"The Pad?" I asked.

"Maxi."

As I stepped into my apartment, Crank intertwined my legs and purred. I pressed a button on the answering machine in the kitchen and opened a can of cat food.

The first message played. "Hey, James, Rick. Sandra's having another party Friday. Give me a call." *Beep.* "James, this is Connie. We're going to O'Hare's tonight. . ."

I looked at the Formica counter lined with empty Dewars bottles.

The next message played. "This is Mr. Daintree from AA. We missed you in group yesterday. Give me a call when you get a chance."

The room spun. Connie's cleavage pouted next to a glass table with lines of cocaine. She laughed in slow motion. New friends sprawled about Anderson's apartment in loosened office attire.

Anderson slapped me on the back. "It's getting late." His words were slow, like a recording played at the wrong speed. "We have to work in the morning."

A man from Pakistan I'd met earlier in the night sat a few feet from the table, typing on the keys of a laptop.

"You a terrorist?" I asked. "Making plans to blow up the city?"

The man scowled and turned the laptop, showing a speedy game of Tetris.

"Maybe I ought to call a cab for super cop," said Anderson.

I jabbed him in the ribs with my finger. "Always feeding on the approval of others."

✝ ✝ ✝

My bed was soft and damp, lukewarm, smelling of beer, brandy, and two kinds of fruit juice. My first thought was water. My second, vomit.

The tone of the answering machine in the kitchen and the voice on the other end pierced my mind. I took in the information. Maxi, steaming. I was late for the meeting.

My brain announced the obvious: you might lose your job—again!

Crank had been eating my vomit. There was a happy cat trail from my bed into the white shag carpeted living room. I looked at the clock: ten fifty-nine.

I scrounged for my cell and called the office. Not Maxi, I thought. Talk to Dana, her assistant. She doesn't hate me—yet.

"Dana?" I asked, helplessly, recognizing Maxi's sharp bark.

"No, James?"

"My grandmother." The moment I spoke the words, I remembered the two women from accounting I'd seen at the second bar we'd hit. Maxi would know.

"Your grandmother?" she repeated.

In my last two jobs, I'd killed off enough family members to be on the FBI's most wanted.

"She died," I said. "I drowned my sorrows in booze." I punched my pillow hard for going with the lamest excuse imaginable.

"You drowned your sorrows in booze?" She repeated my words as though she couldn't believe I'd said them either.

"I'm really not feeling well right now."

"You missed the Prescott meeting."

"Yeah, how did that go?"

"Lousy. Mr. Daintree called for you."

My gastric juices bubbled. "Mr. Daintree?"

"Mr. Daintree from your court-appointed rehab." Her words poked like a needle from the hand of a third-world doctor. "That's the kind of thing you should disclose on a job interview."

My world stopped turning.

"I told him you didn't come in today."

"I can explain."

"I should fire you. Don't call in again." She hung up.

If our lives and souls are made up of our choices, emotions, actions, and words, somewhere the unused possibilities of personhood exist.

—Dionysius, *Enlightened Visions*, 624 A.D.

~ THREE ~

ANDREW II

Sedgwick and I wait, poised on either side of the cell door. My stick legs threaten to collapse beneath me. I can't believe I'm doing this. The lock clicks, and Tremol steps through carrying a food tray. I sack the sheet over his head, push him to the floor, and run from the cell. The old man follows. We're lame mice navigating a stone castle maze. Behind us, Tremol grunts like a wild boar and calls for his brother.

We stop at the head of a mountainous staircase. Tremol's heavy boots round the corner. His voice booms. I cannot think. I'm sure Arrot's sword waits for us at the bottom. We trip and slide. My heart stops. Somehow, we make it down into a large banquet hall. Freedom lies behind a great door. Beyond is life itself. Slivers of sunlight shine through its splintered wood. Amber-and-yellow stained glass gleams above.

Arrot is the last thing I see. His beastly form stands between us and the outside. We're trapped, but I have the advantage: I don't care if I die. I won't live as a slave any longer.

I exchange a look with Sedgwick, hoping beyond hope he has a plan.

Tremol roars. "I'm going to shave the skin off your bones."

In the confusion, I dare not turn around. I run headlong with all my might and crash into a spin on the floor. Furs land around me. It wasn't Arrot but a rack of coats.

A moment later, I feel a thin grip pull me from the floor.

"Run, you damn fool." Sedgwick pushes at my back. He runs ahead and swings open the door.

In an instant, an orgasm of sunlight washes over me, pain tears through my side as Tremol's blade slices.

I scream and catch sight of Sedgwick racing for the gate. I leap off the front steps, holding my side, hot blood on my fingers. Squeezing my wound, I cross the yard on wobbly legs, aiming for the gate Sedgwick disappeared through.

We're among trees, lost in what I'd dreamt of for years. Lie down and die, I think. This place is good enough, but my will doesn't let me. Glimpses of the old man ahead and the cries for Arrot behind force my steps.

We catch our breath together. The gate crashes open fifty yards away and the barbarians hoof in our direction.

Sedgwick leans on me, wheezing. "I'm too weak to go farther."

"You must. I can't go without you."

He points. "There's a chapel on the other side of the valley. Your new life is there." His fingers knife at my arm. "Close the door when you're inside."

A feathered shaft pierces his back. His eye blinks with tears. His hand gives way, and he sinks to his knees.

Arrot and Tremol stand at the edge of a clearing congratulating each other, loading bolts into their crossbows.

Strength leaves me, but I run, forgetting I am mere skin on bones.

An arrow slashes through a tree beside me.

Fortunately, they're gluttons. I gain ground, shambling into the valley, holding my bloody side. Images of the old man's final moments drip senseless in my mind.

A bolt zips past my head.

I look up, and she's there, some distance off, her white countenance glowing under the canopy of trees. She motions to me, an angel to a dying man.

They'll kill her. I'll lead them straight to her.

They're close. My legs and lungs burn. I thrust one narrow foot in front of the other and start the climb to the other side of the valley.

She holds her ground and beckons me.

If people are arrested emotionally and spiritually on one plane of existence, their soul is trapped, and many untapped possibilities of personhood go unused.

—Dionysius, *Enlightened Visions*, 624 A.D.

True forgiveness is the key to enlightenment.

—Dionysius, *Enlightened Visions*, 624 A.D.

~ FOUR ~

JAMES II

I parked along a street at dusk and walked past a half-lit sign reading "Cherry Road School, AA meeting". Inside, I settled into a folding chair near the back of the cafeteria.

Gary, a pot-bellied Vietnam vet with a battalion embroidered hat was at the podium. "One day at a time. For me, it's not just a bumper sticker. I live my life that way."

Mr. Daintree stood beside him for support.

What a waste: addressing a bunch of alcoholics and drug users in a middle school lunch room, trying to tell them something they can actually believe in.

A blond chick with scraggly hair and angel-wing tattoos gave me bedroom eyes. She looked more tortured than the rambling vet. Pretty, sun-soaked blondes are like candy bar wrappers; they're only useful until you eat the candy. As they grow older, they tease their hair because that's all they have left to tease.

People clapped as the vet took his seat, and Mr. Daintree grabbed the microphone. "Thank you. Let's give another hand for Gary. When the ship we're on sinks, it's good to know we can all be on a lifeboat together."

Daintree said this at every meeting. He drilled the symbolism into our addicted minds. I'd rather swim with the sharks than spend my last days starving to death with this lot.

Daintree mingled after the meeting and distributed his life-changing words to people who were barely hanging on. He's the epitome of normal, but then again, anyone shines against such a backdrop. I too have a spot in this family photo, smiling as if I want to be there, properly positioned in the back with the tall men who are sick of life and find their tonic in a bottle of Johnny Walker Red.

I waved to Daintree as though we're old friends. "Do you have a minute?"

He headed for the door. "Actually, I'm running late."

"It's about the call you made to my job."

He stopped and cleared his throat. "There are three people in this group who are required to be here. Last I checked you're one of them. You didn't show last week, so, I called your job."

"Just like that?"

Daintree's jaw tightened. "Just like that."

"This is my life we're talking about."

"I wish you cared more about it. Until you forgive yourself for what happened to your twin brother, you're going to keep drinking."

"That's not fair," I said.

"It's very fair. We want to help you, James."

I stared at the linoleum-squared floor. "I pulled the trigger."

He shook his head. "You were a child. People who can't forgive themselves can't forgive others."

"My grandmother passed away last week." The lie slipped comfortably from my mouth.

He thought about this. "I'm sorry."

"It shook me up."

He nodded. "Does your boss know?"

"Yeah."

"Okay." Halfway through the door, he stopped and looked back. "What step are you on?"

"Eight."

"Forgiveness," he said. "You know, that's the hardest one. See you next week."

The door creaked shut behind him.

This is bullshit. My life is bullshit. I've been on the forgiveness step forever, making lists of people *I've harmed* and scratching them out, ripping the paper into little pieces, and burning those pieces in a tin can on my balcony.

The blond bumped my hip. "Oops. Sorry."

"No problem."

She held out her hand. "Renee."

I took it, noticing her chipped blue fingernail polish. "James."

"Isn't he great?"

I paused and looked at a tattoo of a little man diving headlong into the center of her cleavage. She didn't seem to mind.

"When did you get that?"

"A few years back. I was wasted."

I nodded. Probably not uncommon.

She scrunched her face and formed a smile. "I like it."

I bet you do, I thought. "Does he have a name?"

"Radish."

I scanned the room for a distraction, anyone or anything. "Interesting," I said.

"Named him after one of my ex-boyfriends. He was always . . . well, anyway." She rocked back on her heels. "What step are you on?"

I imagined the glowing embers in my tin can. "Eight."

She scrunched another smile. "My favorite."

"Your favorite?"

"I spend a lot of time on that one."

I looked around the room at the mingling addicts holding overflowing cups of coffee. "Have you been going to meetings long?"

"Feels like it." She leaned in, her mouth an inch from my ear. "You want to know my secret?"

"Sure."

"You'll have to follow me."

I accepted the weight of her breasts against my arm and pressed my thigh against her hip. "Where?"

She curled her index finger and headed for the door. I traced the outline of her hips in her beige cutoffs. This could be good.

Outside, no leaf stirred. The air seemed to hold no temperature, and the city noise was static on the horizon. The sidewalk was a dark path under the trees. She took my hand, pulling me forward.

"Where are we going?"

"My home away from home." She motioned to an old church, dwarfed by the surrounding buildings. Its twin steeples pointed past the haze of city lights to a crescent moon.

I'm disappointed. I'd imagined a van with a waterbed and a disco ball. "I'm not religious."

She brushed the bleached hair from her face. "A little God never hurt anybody."

No, I thought, it was always a big God who did.

An elderly, homeless man wearing a tattered trench coat and a patch over one eye held out his hand. "Spare change?"

I checked my pockets and gave him what I had, though I was a pink slip away from my own bench.

Renee and I entered the church through a wooden door etched with the waves of a river. She pulled the door closed with reverberating finality.

The scents of wood polish and incense carried with them childhood memories: my mother and father walking my twin brother Andrew and me to the pew we decorated every Sunday, until the nightmare of his closed-casket funeral. Though a child, I was old enough to understand I'd never see my best friend again, old enough to know what I'd done and live with it forever.

My legs stopped walking on their own. "What is this place?"

She slid into a pew near the back. "Saint Christopher's Chapel."

I sat down beside her and reached for her bare leg.

"Oh, no. You need to go up there." She guided me toward the front, where the sacristy and pulpit lay sprinkled in candlelight.

On the altar rested a handsome gold cross and an enormous Bible.

I slid my hand up her thigh. "I've come here to be with *you*."

She motioned toward the front. "Just go. Trust me."

This is how it happens, I think. Those people they find bloated and decaying in drainage ditches, they all followed strange women into churches in the middle of the night.

Darkness embraced the corners of the room. I listened hard, but heard only the distant honking of cars outside.

No longer proud of his great size and strength, Reprobus humbled himself, and asked the hermit to assign to him some task by which he might serve God, his master. . . . The hermit led him to a broad and swift river, and said, "Here build thyself a hut, and when wanderers wish to cross, carry them over for the love of Christ." For there was no bridge.

Henceforth, day and night, whenever he was called, Reprobus faithfully performed the task. One night he heard a child calling to be carried across the river. He quickly rose, placed the child on his stout shoulder and walked into the mighty current. The water rose higher and higher, and the child became heavier and heavier.

"O child," he cried, "how heavy thou art! It seems I bear the weight of the world on my shoulder." And the child replied, "Right thou art. Thou bearest not only the world, but The Creator of heaven and earth. I am Jesus Christ, thy King and Lord, and henceforth thou shalt be called Christophorus, that is, Christ-bearer" . . . and the child disappeared.

—Benjamin Clayton, *The History of Saints*, 1867

~ FIVE ~

ANDREW III

The chapel rests near the top of the valley, two jagged steeples against a barren, blue sky. I climb on quivering legs to its threshold.

A calm breeze bathes the forest. My eyes chase the trees' shadows, searching down in the valley for the woman in white, Tremol, and Arrot.

I see what I fear most. They've pinned her against a tree. Arrot presses his forearm against her neck and the thick blade of his sword to her belly.

I look away, wishing a quick death for us both. Yet, with a second's worth of courage, I turn the knob and barrel past a door etched with waves into the chapel in search of a weapon.

Somehow, I will find a way to save the woman in white.

I stumble into black. The smells of damp earth and ancient wood mix. As my eyes adjust, I see a woman sitting to my right and a man standing near a candlelit altar. On the altar sits a handsome gold cross and an enormous Bible.

"Help her! Please!" I collapse.

A thunderstorm rages in my mind. I stare from where I lie at the carvings in the dimly lit ceiling. A beautiful blond woman nestles my head in her lap and smiles down at me.

I think it might be the woman in white, but her hair is too yellow, her skin marked.

"Am I dead?" I wonder aloud.

"Who's this?"

I sit up at the sound of a familiar voice.

A man steps from the darkness. He looks just like me. Same dark blond hair, same sharp cheekbones, and same wide jaw.

He jumps back. "Who the hell are you?"

We both look to the woman.

Memories flood back. I try to rise, but the woman keeps me down.

"There's a woman in the woods. I need to save her." Tears fill my eyes. "She may already be dead."

"There's no woods around here," says the man who looks like me.

The chapel door crashes open, letting in the blinding afternoon sun. Two beastly silhouettes stand twenty yards from us in the doorway.

The woman springs to her feet.

"Who are these two?" asks the man who looks like me. "How can it be daytime?"

Tremol grabs the handle and slams the door shut.

"Don't!" cries the woman. She tugs on my shoulder and calls to the man who looks like me. "Come on, James!"

"Looks like we got ourselves some gophers hidin' in a church," spits Tremol.

James steps forward. "Just a minute, I'm sure—"

An arrow flashes across the room and sticks in the wall beside him. James jumps, eyes round and white in the dim chapel.

Arrot chortled. "Shut your mouth."

James runs to meet us in the room behind the altar. The woman leads us through a narrow-walled tunnel. We follow her into the dark.

James pushes in beside me. "What the hell's going on?"

"Quiet." The woman quickly lifts boards from the floor and nudges me toward the hole.

I ease myself down. The man and woman slip in beside me, and she replaces the planks. The three of us huddle in a shallow pit.

The killers' feet shuffle to a stop overhead, in the little room where the passage ends, making sand and gravel rain on us.

Through the slits in the floorboards, I make out a bulky figure right above us. Candlelight darts about the room.

Tremol edges forward. "Now, come on. No use hidin'."

"Hold on," says Arrot, "the tunnel ends here."

Tremol spins round. "Then where'd they go?"

Arrot points toward the floor.

"Hello?" Someone calls from far off in the chapel.

The two look at each other.

Arrot leads the way. "Come on. They're not goin' anywhere."

Tremol stomps on the floor above us, letting us know we're trapped.

We crouch in our pre-made grave, listening to our own breathing, not daring to move.

Sweat drips down my forehead. My heart aches for another chance to save the woman in white and now myself. I curse myself for running. I should have sacrificed myself to save her with no weapon at all. I wonder why she came to me.

My mind tries to unlock the puzzle of the strange man who looks like me, now huddled inches away in the dark. What are he and this woman doing in this chapel in the wood?

Eventually, she slides the planks hiding us out of the way and hoists herself up. We follow. James and I grab boards from the floor to use as weapons.

We step, careful not to make a sound and strain to hear down the tunnel.

The woman presses her ear against the door leading to the back of the chapel and edges it open. The board trembles in my hands.

We step into an empty sanctuary. The front door stands open, exposing the night outside.

"Night again?" James says.

"How can it be dark?" I ask. We hadn't hidden that long.

The woman heads for the door. Beside it, near the back row of pews, Sedgwick lies dead. A bolt sticks through a bloody wound in his chest. I run to his side. Only this was not Sedgwick, though he looks much the same. He's dressed in a long tattered coat and has a patch covering his foul eye.

The woman weeps and sits on the floor holding him.

James paces. "This is insane. We need to call the police. Do you have a cell?"

The woman rocks the body in her arms. "Horrible."

"Damn right," James shouts.

The woman's gaze is lost. "They've crossed over."

I lift the patch on the man's eye and let it snap back down. The wound is the same as Sedgwick's.

James cautiously spies outside. "I have a phone in my car. I'll call for help."

The woman doesn't answer, and he hurries into the night.

"What do you mean 'crossed over'?" I ask.

Her eyes meet mine. "This is the world of the living. You didn't shut the door to the world of the dead."

My stomach knots as I try to assimilate her words. I shift my gaze to the headlights of a truck passing by outside and rush to the entrance. "My, God. It's all different."

Lamps glow on a street lined with cars. In the distance, over rows of houses and apartments, skyscrapers chisel their modern shapes into the skyline.

This can't be right.

I stumble back. "What is this place? What's happening?"

She leaves her friend on the floor and helps me into a pew. "I'm Renee. I know this must be confusing." Her eyes wander to the candles burning at the altar. "New things so often are." She puts her head in her hands and sighs. "It wasn't supposed to be like this."

"What?"

A half-smile grows on her lips. "Your rapture, Andrew."

"What do you mean? How do you know me?"

"Sedgwick was your Helper," she says. "I'm also a Helper. The Order's been watching you for years."

The man returns holding his chest and panting. "The police are on their way."

Renee stands and places a comforting hand on my shoulder. "And what are you going to tell them, James?"

He pauses in disbelief. "That man's dead . . . and we were nearly killed!"

"I don't understand." I weep. "What happened to the forest? Where am I?"

"There's nothing the police can do," Renee says gently.

James throws his arms in the air. "They can catch those men. What if someone saw us come in here. We can't run, we'll go to jail for sure."

She looks at us both. "No, they can't. We have to go after them."

He steps back. "What are you talking about? I'm not going after anybody."

"Your life has a purpose you don't understand yet," Renee says.

James rubs his forehead. "You drag me over here in the middle of the night, and suddenly I'm getting shot at with *arrows*. These guys kill a bum, you seem to know, and we barely escape with our lives."

Panic overtakes my body. "Where am I? Who are you people?"

James points at me. "Calm down. You're at Maple and Genesee. I'm on a bad trip. I need a drink."

"There's no time to explain," Renee pats my shoulder and walks toward James. "Those aren't ordinary men. They've crossed over to let evil into this world."

James makes for the door. "You're both crazy."

Renee follows him. "If we don't stop them, they'll introduce an evil into the world beyond anything you can imagine."

"Tell that to the cops."

† † †

I fall asleep in Renee's car while James speaks to the police. When I wake, we're moving and James is peering back at me, the way you look at yourself in a mirror when you don't like what you were seeing.

Renee stops a silver medallion from swinging on the rearview mirror. "You know in your heart it's true."

James shakes his head. "The only thing I know is I almost died tonight, and the police think we killed a homeless guy."

Renee turns left. "He wasn't homeless. He was a Helper like me."

The car squeals to a stop across the street from a massive cathedral with gargoyles perching on its gilded corners. We get out and cross the street to a rundown efficiency attached to the parsonage.

"What are you, a preacher's daughter or something?" asks James with a sneer. "We're going to do blow in a church?"

Renee unlocks the door of her quaint home and ushers us in. "Something better."

Tapestries with rich hues of maroon and gold cover the walls of the apartment, spilling onto the floor. Each rug is embroidered with the intricate patterns of labyrinths and hieroglyphics.

James eyes the counter. "What do you have to drink?"

"Help yourself." Renee disappears into a bedroom.

James checks the fridge and cabinets. "Nothing."

He paces from the glass-topped table to the beaten, brown La-Z-Boy in the corner. "The cops want us for further questioning. You know what that means don't you? It means we're suspects."

Renee returns carrying a parchment. "Clean and sober." She unrolls the ancient-looking paper and lays it on the table.

James forces a brittle smile. "What's this?"

She taps on the paper. "Silva somnium desolo, The Forest of Forgotten Dreams."

My insides melt and drain to my feet. "Is that where I was? It's on your map?"

James looks over Renee's shoulder. "What the hell are you talking about?"

"It's hard to explain," Renee answers, holding my gaze. "You were in a place beyond this world."

"This guy isn't from *The Forest of Forgotten Dreams*," James says. "That's ridiculous. Do you have any blow or not?"

"James, why do you think he's here?" Renee asks. "Do you think this is just a coincidence?"

"No. I think he wants to get high. No offense, but it doesn't look like the guy's eaten in months." He slides a business card on a table and makes his way to the door. "I told the cops we'd be at the station in the morning. See you then."

"You don't believe because of what you think you know about this world," says Renee.

"I know I'd better be at work tomorrow."

Renee's demeanor softens. "Your job's changed. You have something more important to do."

James stops at the door, his hand on the knob. "What are you talking about?"

She points at the map. "Give me five minutes. Don't turn your back on your destiny. What if there's a reason for all the pain you've endured? What if your suffering had a purpose?"

He walks slowly back to the table and scowls at the map. "I must be stupid."

She leans over the parchment littered with splotchy ink circles and interconnecting lines.

"Have you ever heard of Reprobus?"

I shook my head.

"Is that for restless leg syndrome?" James asks. "I can't believe I'm listening to this."

"Saint Christopher," Renee continues, "is the patron saint of travel. This is the map he was given by God."

I trace the age-old lines with my finger. "What are these?"

"They show gateways to other worlds. Do you two believe in heaven?"

"When I was a child," James snaps. "Heaven and hell are for children."

"I don't know," I admit.

Renee points to a miniscule circle on the paper with three symbols and lines stitching from it. "This is it."

James snorts, peering over Renee's shoulder to the tiny spot on the paper. "It's really something."

I examine the cryptic markings. "Why is it so much smaller than the others?"

She shrugs. "Don't know. I've never been."

James sinks his hands into his jean pockets. "You just haven't met the right man yet."

Renee rolls her eyes and points to another circle. "We're here: The Mortal Plane."

"You know," James says, "you may want to look into some other groups, like Insanity Anonymous. Mr. Mysterious here can join you."

Renee traces a line on the map with her finger. "Fine, I'll show you. We can get to Zenith quite easily."

"Isn't that a TV?" James asks. "Do you plan on traveling via DVD?"

I grip the edges of the table. "This must be real. I have no other reason for being here."

"'Because you have seen me'," Renee says, "'you have believed; blessed are those who have not seen and yet have believed.'"

James heads for the door and yanks it open. "I guess I'm not blessed, because I'm out of here."

Renee rolls up the map. "Those weren't men at the chapel tonight."

"She's right," I say. "They held me prisoner in another place—a horrible place. Things were different there."

James stands with one foot poised in the still night outside. "Different how?"

"Like when you're asleep . . . and you're waking up, and things don't seem quite real."

"OxyContin," he says, wringing his hands. "I need a drink."

Renee strolls to the door and gently touches his arm. "Let me show you something."

"I've seen enough!"

She takes his hand in hers. "Please."

We follow her into the courtyard of the church and then through an unlocked side door. The sanctuary smells of wood polish and incense. Our steps echo against the cathedral ceiling. Stained glass washes the expansive room in blue and maroon.

Renee stands before the altar and bows her head, mumbling.

"If someone starts shooting arrows," James says, "I'm out of here."

"Quiet," I say. "I think she's praying."

Balmy air blasts into the church without a knowable source. The wind increases to deafening and whirls around us.

James holds fast to a pew, hair and clothes blowing. "What's happening?"

I try to speak, but invisible hands lift me from the ground.

Silence invades.

We're transported to another place, perhaps another time, outside on a sunny spring day, surrounded by behemoth stones standing on end. On every side of the hill, evergreen forest layers the land. Birds chatter.

I stand motionless for a long time, fighting a feeling of helplessness.

James holds his hands out before him as though what he sees is on a screen he'll run into. He drops to his hands and knees. "Okay. What's going on?"

Rence stands before a giant slab of rock in the center of the stone pillars. "Zenith," she announces, proudly.

Having escaped from eternal rape, I really don't care that I'm traveling from world to world. I don't care about the poor, unbelieving fool who looks like me, groveling on the ground, muttering to himself.

I think back to the woman in white's demise and calculate my cowardice. I remember Sedgwick, my Helper, who gave me the will to escape, something I'd been unable to find on my own. I dig deep to rekindle this strength.

James feels the rough stones and plucks the sparse, yellow flowers scattered among the gravel. A warm wind touches us in passing. Renee shoots a smile in my direction. In this setting, she looks almost noble.

"Why are we here?"

"Sometimes it's easier if you see things for yourself."

"No. Why are we *here*?"

She tilts her head to one side. "What, in the big picture?"

I nod, afraid I don't want to know, feeling certain I have a place I belong—a family to return to.

She looks toward the distant, snowcapped mountains for a moment, and then she meets my gaze. "Andrew, like James, you've suffered."

Bowing my head, I acknowledged the truth of her words.

"But, it isn't all for nothing. You're here to save the world."

Her words take hold of me like a parent saving a child from a fire. In the shadow of the rock, Renee looks less worn by life.

"There was a woman in The Forest of Forgotten Dreams who looked like you," I say.

"Did she?"

I nod.

She steps out of the shadow, into the beaming spring mountain light and grabs my narrow hips. Something about her is unreachable, like when the woman in white was at the outer gate or at the top of the valley.

"To the untrained eye," she whispers, "we all look alike."

I notice the tattoo on her chest, a little man diving into the chasm of her bosom. All hope of her being the woman in white flutters from my mind.

"That's Radish," she says. "He likes boobs."

I look around the stones. "Where's James?"

† † †

We peer into the gloomy woods and call out.

Renee takes me by the arm and whispers in my ear. "Do you know what Zenith means?"

I say nothing.

"It means the high point. But, God's not here." She looks me in the eyes. "It's not safe. We need you both." She raises her voice. "James!"

The birds stop chirping. All becomes still. Then they explode from the trees into the cloudless sky and dive once again into the safety of the leaves and branches.

"We must find him before night. Come on." She strides toward the forest.

I'm not anxious to enter, but I hurry behind, trying to keep up. And before I know it, we're under a disorienting canopy of trees, tripping through shrubs, scraping our shoulders on bark, calling to a frantic and lost alcoholic.

A thousand scratches and hours later, we find him huddling on the other side of a river—a madman, a drenched, wild animal.

He looks like I feel.

Renee steps into the river. Her sandals slip on the stone bed.

"Stay back!" James stands.

"Damn it, James." She points at me. "Can't you see who this is?"

Who am I? I don't even know myself.

"This is your brother, Andrew!"

My breath sticks to my lungs.

James looks up and sobs in convulsions. "Stop fucking with me! Andrew's dead."

"He's right here."

I almost believe her.

Renee inches deeper into the rippling, cool water. "Why don't you tell your twin how you killed him."

James wails, turning himself inside out in tears.

Renee glances at the sky and lowers her voice. "It's getting dark. Let's go back to the church, and I'll explain everything."

James steadies himself on a pine sapling. "You're a witch!"

Renee stops. "I assure you I'm not."

"He can't be Andrew. My brother died when he was eight." James turns and runs, dodging branches, vanishing into the wood.

"James, stop!" she calls after him, but it's no use.

I sit where the water pulses against the smooth, black stones that line the shore, overwhelmed by my short life. "But, I thought once someone died—"

"You're alive," Renee snaps, "but none of us will be if we don't find that idiot." She edges across the river. "Come on."

"So, what happened to me?" I ask. "I died when I was eight?"

She steps past the first line of trees on the other side. "Come on!"

"I need to know," I scream. "What happened to me?"

Water laps near my trembling feet. I turn my gaze to the last rays of yellow light above the shimmering trees, the sun sliding behind the treetops and wonder if I'm dead.

✝ ✝ ✝

Dusk smolders the world around us. Renee and I rest between two boulders under low-lying branches. Strangely, I long for the safety of my prison. I wonder how long I was locked up and rotting away. Pain-filled memories swim into the moment, reminding me of what was lost: my parents, brother, and childhood.

Her hand creeps up my thigh. "If I hadn't given up smoking," she says, "I'd have matches to start a fire. I guess it's for the best, we wouldn't want to alert anything we're here."

"Anything like what?"

Only the wind answers, swaying tree branches. Birds sing their final songs for the day.

"Anything like what?" I ask again.

"Anything at all," she swallows and scans the shadowy outline of trees. "This is one of the old worlds, a place where creatures that used to be people live. They'd love to sacrifice us to their gods."

"What do you mean? Kill us?"

She nods. "There were many worlds before the one you were born in, and many people before your people."

The forest seems eerily calm.

"James is lost and hiding in the woods," Renee brushes a twig from my hair. "The thing is . . . he's only hiding from himself." She inches closer so that our bodies touch. "That's what people do, you know. They hide from themselves."

She smells like an exotic flower, something far away and expensive.

I try to say, "I'm scared," but the warmth of her mouth smothers my words.

My thoughts stutter at the sudden advance.

Her sweet breath surrounds me in the darkness. Her whispers caress my ears. I drop my head in search of her breasts.

She speaks softly. "You're only a child."

I find her towering mounds, smelling of tender flesh and roses. "I don't believe I was dead."

She cranes her neck to clamp my earlobe between her teeth. "Only the soulless are truly dead."

My heart leaps into the emptiness of her words.

"Hold me."

I reach for her, but she feels countries away.

"Hold me," she pleads.

I press against her as tightly as I can manage, laying my face against her candy-satin hair, but I still feel more alone than ever. "I don't understand."

She pushes me away. "I'm not like you," she whispers. "I don't have a soul. I'm only a possibility in someone else's life."

I fight for air and comprehension.

She stills. "Do you hear that?"

"I don't hear anything," I mutter.

She grabs my arms with new strength. "There are fates worse than death. You should know that."

Something cracks branches with heavy steps.

My voice gives away my fear. "What is it?"

"Shut up."

We are motionless, watching moon-fed shadows slink against the backdrop of trees. My body tells me to run, but Renee's hand holds fast to my arm. In an instant, we're surrounded by larger-than-life figures, darker than the night itself.

Something strikes my chest, and I double over in pain, gasping.

They lash our hands and feet to staffs and carry us—game from a hunt. I shudder to think where they might be taking us. I call to Renee, but she doesn't answer.

They stop and lay us on rocks.

For the first time, I see our hooded captors. Their faces resemble those of wild hogs. Sniffing snouts protrude from their midnight black robes. My body shudders uncontrollably as hope abandons me.

The sun creeps into daylight and exposes the world's grittiness. In the distance, across the waves of long grass, I see the hill of Zenith surrounded by a sea of black-hooded figures.

I call to Jesus, and the pigmen retort with squeals, raising their snouts to the emerging sky. I call to Renee and I'm cracked against my skull.

✝ ✝ ✝

Renee sleeps soundly among the stones of Zenith, still bound, only feet away. A chorus of snorting surrounds us.

Two pigmen sling James onto the rock altar like a slab of meat.

The phrase "Fates worse than death" echoes through my battered head.

I call to James, and he lifts his head, shakily. I hide my eyes from the sight. Teeth stick through the flesh surrounding his mouth, nestled in a bloody concoction of swollen eyes, hair, and raw meat.

The grunting intensifies. Thousands of hooves stomp in unison.

In the very center of the circle, an immense pigman holds a tri-bladed knife over James.

The pounding slows.

Silence spreads.

I long for salvation beyond hope for us all, but once again I am helpless to save.

Patches open among the pigmen masses. They back away from black piles of cloth that rise to life. Nuns spring up in black-and-white dress.

The creatures cower making guttural noises. Seven nuns march toward Zenith, where we lie helpless. They lift machine guns, and the pigmen scatter, squealing.

The knife falls into James.

He wails.

Guns crack.

A spray of bullets sends the leader of the pigmen into a spastic dance. Bloody pieces fly.

To have imagination is to be able to see the world in its totality, for the power and the mission of the Images is to show all that remains refractory to the concept: hence the disfavor and failure of the man "without imagination"; he is cut off from the deeper reality of life and from his own soul.

—Mircea Eliade

Imagination is more important than knowledge.

—Albert Einstein

~ SIX ~

JAMES III

I was worse off than I'd imagined. My pounding head, cuts, and bruises were surpassed by the burning in my gut where the knife had entered.

My aching hand instinctively reached for the pocket where I kept minibottles of gin. Instead, I found a vulnerably-open cotton hospital gown. I tried to swear, but my mouth had been stitched, bandaged on one side, and crammed full of blood-coated gauze. I choked back the cotton lining.

The room swam in the light of a single dim bulb hanging from the ceiling. The plaster walls were bare, except for a looming crucifix. The savior's skin painted the color of real flesh. I felt his disapproval and agony. A painting on the far wall showed the Virgin Mary cradling her infant son—a reminder of the innocence to cruelty that awaits us all.

I eased myself from the bed, limped toward the heavy brown drapes, and doubled over on the sill. Outside, a lively group of nuns crossed the courtyard below. On the horizon, lavender, snowcapped mountains pinnacled.

I dabbed at my battered face with the edge of the gown.

This is the worst trip I've ever had. I wondered if Renee slipped PCP into my AA coffee.

An abrupt knock sounded and a mousy nun entered. She stopped suddenly when she saw me awake.

My wounds pulsed with anguish. Each syllable tore my cheek. "Where am I?"

She spoke with an accent I couldn't place. "Please, rest. Everything will be explained in time."

"No!" I tore my stitches and felt scorching pain. "Where am I? I want to leave!"

Blood filled my mouth.

The nun rushed to the door and called for help.

✝ ✝ ✝

The clergy gave me a shot that shunned my thoughts and made my body ice-water numb. The nun pushed me in an antique wheelchair down long stone corridors and into a monastery chapel packed with monks, nuns, and priests.

A stout woman with cropped black hair and a Rosary in one hand addressed the group. She raised her pudgy arms with passion. "We must attack them, not wait for them to defeat us!"

A reedy priest pushed the mop-gray hair from his eyes. "Mother Adair, we don't even know that Mastema has been awakened. Why would you think such evil would come here? How could God allow it?"

"I need a drink," I slurred.

Clergy sitting nearby shot concerned glances.

Mother Adair looked right at me. "Perhaps there are some here who live in wishes and dreams. They may think: Why would our world change when things have been this way for so long? But those who study reality know change is inevitable."

The clergy grumbled.

A beer with a whisky chaser would hit the spot, I thought.

Mother Adair balled her fists. "The Helpers tell us Arrot and Tremol may have already contacted Mastema. No need to tell you what would happen if that evil is born into this world. We must strike before they breach any other worlds."

Everyone gasped.

I noticed "my brother" staring at me from several pews away. The possibility that Andrew was alive completed my torture and breathed life into my suffocating heart. I sat on my shaking hands.

After the meeting, the room cleared, and I was left with Mother Adair, my malnourished lookalike, and Renee, with her tattoos, now dressed like a nun. I'd always run into trouble chasing ass, but this was beyond hellish.

Mother Adair placed a soothing hand on my shoulder. "Poor child. It's by God's providence you're alive." She turned to Renee. "You're here with no thanks to your Helper. She's not even here. Instead, she sent this possibility."

"Head Mother," Renee said, "please—"

"Silence. We may have war because of your failures."

I hadn't noticed the bum sitting in a nearby pew. I was surprised to see him alive, dressed like a priest, and wearing a patch over one eye.

He looked as though the weight of the world were on him. He spoke with a raspy voice. "However I may serve, Head Mother."

Mother Adair rubbed the beads on her Rosary. "Have the twins been given their briefing?"

"There was no time," answered Renee.

Mother Adair made white-knuckled fists. "But, you had time to go to Zenith and almost lose one of the pairs in a forbidden world to godless creatures?

"Sorry, Head Mother. I thought showing them Zenith would prove the existence—"

Mother Adair slammed her fist against the pew. "Have you learned nothing? You cannot force belief! Only choose candidates who already believe. Must I keep reiterating your role as Helpers? Find twins, the potential Witnesses, school and test them! They must believe or we are wasting time."

The malnourished lookalike said, "I believe."

Everyone looked at him in gratitude and then at me. They waited. I stared back, boggled.

"He's been injured," Renee said. "Let him heal."

"We have no time. The wolf is at the gate. Ready them." Mother Adair stormed from the room.

My anorexic "brother" inched closer to the one-eyed priest and called to him. "Sedgwick?"

The priest turned to Renee. "It's time."

We followed him through halls bustling with clergy. Some looked like Renee, others like the one-eyed priest, and many others were different altogether with pale skin and long, thin Nordic faces or the high cheekbones of Eastern Europeans.

We entered an old-world room lined with archaic books, odd compasses, and navigational instruments on pedestals.

The one-eyed priest tromped to the far side of the small room. "What does each of you remember of your previous life?"

I battled my groggy state, trying to shake the nausea and stand. I knew if I could get out of the wheelchair I could escape.

The lookalike said, "Only the prison, Sedgwick. Weren't you there?"

"That wasn't me," said the priest.

"Then, who was it? Do you have a brother as well?" The lookalike glanced my way.

An emotional stew boiled in my stomach.

The priest leaned his thin hip on an antique desk. "Sedgwick was one of your Helpers, just as I am. He was one of my possibilities. Renee is one of your brother's Helpers."

Renee stood behind me and gripped the wheelchair handles. "We must hurry."

The priest marched to the window and faced us, silhouetted. "Reconsider what makes you Andrew and James Blight."

"That's not Andrew Blight!" I tore my stitches and tasted blood.

The priest turned to me. "Have you ever said or done anything because you were scared, angry, happy or jealous?"

"Of course," answered the lookalike.

"When you remember these times," the priest said, "have you ever questioned if that was you? Why doesn't it *feel* like you? Your soul dances through emotional states, whirling through a trillion possibilities." His arms opened wide—a deranged evangelist. "These are streams on the space time continuum."

I rubbed my head and looked at the table, overwhelmed by the insanity of it all.

The priest wheeled out an antiquated reel-to-reel projector on a cart and turned it on. He flipped a button that lowered a screen on the far wall of the room. "I don't know if you're familiar with quantum physics, but this was way before its time."

A black-and-white movie played, taking a man in the nineteen-fifties through his day: waking in the morning, eating eggs and toast with his family, driving to work in a Studebaker. Through the day, he encountered choices and emotions: forgiveness for his daughter after spilling orange juice on his slacks, happiness at sharing a meal with his family, and anger at a coworker's negligence.

The audio was a Disneyesque tune with narration: "Who are you when you wake in the morning? How about a second later?

"We're told we have a forgiving side, a vengeful side, a side that loves, and a side that despises. Because you're multiples and you share the same soul, the rules are different for you. Your soul lives outside your body. This creates a new plane of existence where your emotional states are beings all their own. Every slight variation makes a new 'you.' This happens to everyone, only for everyone else these 'you's' are on the inside. Your possibilities exist in the physical reality we all share. To begin this process you must only cross into another world.

"Who are you this instant? Who will you be tomorrow? If you're a twin or more, these states of being exist with or without your soul.

"Choices, emotions, actions, and words are elements of personhood, but who is that person? Modernists unite these things with our physical form, because their understanding is limited to this plane of existence.

"Truth is the multiple's soul, your soul, thrives in worlds beyond imagination, dancing from one layer of reality to the next, finding its identity beyond your personhood."

The movie showed the narrator, a clean-cut man in a black suit and tie, standing beside a pigtailed girl on a swing under the shady branches of a maple tree. He started her with a push, and she kicked high into the air.

"There are untapped 'persons'," the narrator said. "Possibilities our souls never use."

The projector reel spun round, until the screen darkened and blasted white with light.

The priest flipped off the projector. "Of course, this film and what I've said is meant for students who are further along. I've no doubt you're confused. But, we don't have the time to—"

I slammed the side of the wheelchair with my fists. "What the hell are you talking about? Let me out of here!"

The others looked shocked.

I hung my head. "I didn't ask for this."

"We never ask for what life brings," Renee said, with a schoolteacher's even stare. "This is your destiny."

"What's the problem?" asked the one-eyed priest.

Blood slimed down my throat and dripped off the edge of my chin. "Are you serious?"

The priest pointed to the window. "You've already done a great service for God."

Renee wheeled me over, and I peered into the courtyard below.

Reality unraveled. For an instant, I felt nothing at all.

A thousand men wearing the ashen-brown robes of monks, holding massive, black mechanized guns stood in formation. Their faces were identical to my own—before mine had been pulverized.

The man Renee claimed was my brother stood beside me, sharing the same shocked expression.

The priest strolled over and gave a thin-lipped smile. "God allows the chosen to use even their regrets to fight evil. These secrets are self-evident to multiples. We fight evil with the untapped soulless parts of a person."

The lookalike scowled at the monk army. "That doesn't make sense."

The priest pressed the button to raise the screen. "Some believe spiritual warfare is metaphorical. In actuality it's quantum."

The door behind us opened, and the gray-mop-haired priest from earlier said, "We're leaving."

In spite of the local appearances of phenomena, our world is actually supported by an invisible reality which is unmediated and allows communication faster than light, even instantaneously.

—McEvoy, J.P., and Zarate, *Introducing Quantum Theory*, 1996

~ SEVEN ~

ANDREW IV

I find his room at the end of a hallway. A lone nun, wielding a snub-nose machine gun guards its entrance. I wonder if she's there to protect him or to keep him from leaving. She lets me by.

I knock lightly on the inside of the door. "Hello?"

There's no answer, so I step to the side of his bed. "Everyone's gone. They vanished in the church."

James lies still, staring at the plastered ceiling above his bed.

I wince at the sight of him. "Renee told me to see you. She says a great evil is coming to kill all the multiples . . . that means you and me." Silence fills the room. "Are you really my brother?"

James slides up in bed with a moan. "That's impossible," he mutters, "but with all that's happened. . . . What do you remember?"

"Not much," I admit. My mind still seems lost in The Forest of Forgotten Dreams.

"Christmas?" James says the word as if it contains a world in itself. And, it does.

My heart takes hold—a child reaching for the arms of its nourishing mother. *Christmas* brings with it warm scents and presents, faceless relatives, and a home.

My face must have brightened.

"I guess it may be true," he says, studying me. "You might be Andrew."

"Is that who I am?"

He tries to sit up but finds it too difficult. "You and a thousand others in the courtyard." He coughs. "I don't even care who those men are. I just want to get the hell out of here." He dabs the blood at the side of his mouth with the sheet.

I clear my throat, unsure of what to say. If this is my brother, maybe I truly had died. I reach for him, either to hug or strangle—I'm not sure which. Emotional towers collapse to rubble within me. "What happened when we were children?"

He looks up at me, his eyes as shattered as his body. "I shot you. We were eight."

I lose sight of his eyes in the pooling tears. I'm not sure if they're mine or his. I think they're ours.

"I killed you," he says.

Words fail me, as does my heart and body and all of life.

Moments later, when the church bell tolls outside, my conscience buzzes like a million purpose-driven bees. They're building something sweet inside me.

I peer out the window, hoping to see the reason for the alarm, but the courtyard's vacant. I hear tapping outside the door and race to answer it. The nun's gone. Down the hall, a kaleidoscope of light and shadow struggles against the stone wall. Panicked wails and a woman's muffled scream sound. My eyes dart to the wheelchair in the corner of the room, and then to the battered form of my brother.

✝ ✝ ✝

I curse the squeaky wheel that echoes down every dim corridor we pass. I push James fast, hoping to find safety outside. A new feeling grows in my guts, as I try to save my twin who sent me to my personal hell.

The nun lies in the center of the hall. The weight of her body presses on her broken neck and contorted face. Her child-bearing thighs stretch toward the towering ceiling. Blood-red marks are cut into the fabric of her uniform and her pale flesh below. A veiny umbilical cord winds round one filleted leg, down the passage, and around the lightless corner.

James reaches over his shoulder and grips my wrist.

I turn us back the way we came, but before I take a step, the sound of a billion scurrying legs envelopes us. The walls turn slick black with centipedes, and at the end of the hall, behind us, the shadow of a figure swells.

Hot urine trickles down my leg.

A child rounds the corner, a nude boy holding the strand of his umbilical cord. He takes the methodical steps of a young hunter.

James strikes my hand repeatedly trying to get my attention.

The boy looks confused. He holds back tears and then gushes; wailing and holding up the cord.

He's upon us, standing at our feet. His mouth opens wide in the throes of sickness. A thousand centipedes rattle out.

We race, trying to outrun their clicking legs. Turning the corner, the wheelchair catches on a rock. James spills headfirst onto the floor. The chair clatters end over end.

James lets out an agonized scream and tries to lift himself in the midst of the impenetrable barrage of insects.

Doom creeps over the cells of our skin, fondling our helpless bodies. I shake, trying to rid myself of its presence.

I see the double doors of the church, grab James under the arms, close my eyes, and yank his deadweight through the entrance. The candle-laden chapel is filled with gold leaf and statuary.

James squirms free and tests his legs.

The doors explode off their hinges. A bluster of decay blows in from the pitch-black hall.

I turn to the altar where the clergy had vanished and pray fervently for us to be transported.

Nothing happens.

The boy appears from the darkness of the hall. He drags the mousy nun's corpse like a ball and chain and peers greedily into the chapel. He's larger now than moments before, licking his lips, making way for the thousand-legged insects fleeing his mouth.

James gurgles unintelligible pleas.

"Jesus, please help us!" I yell.

The child pauses and looks around the room, twisting his head like a curious dog. The room flickers into a red, broiling furnace. Waves of heat bear down, smashing us to the floor. My blood boils within me.

The boy chatters. Gold melts off crosses, art, and trim; dripping to the marble floor and streaming toward his adolescent body. His face is narrow-lined. His nose, cheekbones, and chin unnaturally pointy. The sides of his mouth turn up—a demented clown. His blazing eyes hold all fury.

The nun's corpse shrivels on the ground beside him.

Shots ring. All around us, the clergy fires. The barrage chips stone.

The presence stands, unscathed. He raises his long, pale hand. Every pew, statue, and person flies against the back wall, smashing together with head-crushing pressure. Furniture and statuary strike unforgiving blows.

New clergy appear in thin air, fire, and flutter back into the fray.

A priest smashes against the wall. He fights to raise his gun and blasts rounds into the shriveled nun's remains. They splatter like an insect underfoot. The presence, now a full-grown man, grunts like a speared bull and rips the cord from his stomach.

At once, the contents of the church collapse to the floor. An unearthly screech drowns the clergy's mumbling chants.

The searing red heat is replaced with transcendent, white light.

I come to and struggle to stand. In every direction, the dunes of a desert meet with the horizon. The bodies of priests, nuns, and monks, both alive and dead are piled in a row. Many look like me. The lamenting cries of survivors fill the air.

I find James, his head crushed by a statue of Saint Peter. I collapse onto the sand beside him and stare into the unforgiving sky. The sun scorches my retinas, but I don't care if I go blind. What little will to live I'd recovered is gone.

Renee stands over me, casting her shadow on my face. "You all right?"

My own head feels crushed along with my brother's. I wish it were.

She helps me to my feet.

Among the murmurings, someone yells, "Mother Adair is dead!"

Cries of grief follow. Few remain alive.

"He's dead," I howl. "I barely knew him."

Renee takes my hand.

I glance at what's left of my brother and jerk my head away. "He's dead."

Renee holds me tight, pressing her body close. "If you're not dead, he's not dead. Multiple births share the same soul. If one of you dies you live on in another world."

For a moment, I'm lost in the embrace, and tune out the screams of regret. I latch onto my own faulty resolve.

"We tracked Arrot and Tremol into the first layer of hell," Renee says. "We needed to return them to the forest to set things right. But, they were waiting. Now evil is out, and only the true Witnesses of God can stop it."

My brother's remains flash in my mind's eye. The resilience behind Renee's gaze pulls me closer. I feel like an unhinged marionette in a playhouse—useless and disconnected. The clergy call for survivors as they pick through the wreckage and heinous discoveries.

Renee pulls her hand free. "We're doomed. They're going to cut God off from the world."

"Cut off God?" My eyes wander to a group of priests with rosaries hanging from their necks. They crouch next to fierce weapons, long-barreled machine guns, the same I'd seen unleashed on the pigs.

"Isn't God all powerful?" I ask.

Renee shields her eyes from the sun. "In a sense."

"We need to move," a gray-bearded monk calls out, "it's a three-day journey to the Ridge Tower."

Whirling desert wind follows his words, as the condemning teeth of reality sink deep into those who remain. We have no water and no supplies.

"We're lost." A sand-speckled priest observes.

"God has forsaken us," shouts another.

I search my heart and find a baseless hope. "There must be a way!"

A group of priests dismiss me with a wave. "He doesn't know his calling. He's only a new twin."

Renee grabs my arm and takes me to the side. "Evil moves faster than good. They'll cut God off from the human plane before we're able to mount a fight. All that's left is to defend heaven."

The survivors crowd around.

"We must fight for heaven," shouts someone.

Renee hangs her head. "The soulless cannot enter heaven. We're the unchosen paths."

I scan their desperate faces. "I don't understand."

"How can it be his destiny?" yells someone.

The group starts to walk away, shaking their heads.

I pull Renee to my side. "Tell me what I need to know. What are they talking about?"

Her eyes reflect the vacant desert and give nothing back. "You may be the last twin," she says. "It's up to you to save the world."

CHRISTOPHER HAWKE

The wolf will live with the lamb, the leopard will lie down with the goat, the calf and the lion and the yearling together; and a little child will lead them.

—*The New International Version Bible*, Isaiah 11:6

ANDREW V

My heart grieves a past and brother I barely knew, while my mind focuses desperately on the hope of a future. Tomorrow seems ripe for the taking in a way too obvious to be good, with promised threats yet unimagined. I wonder if a search for James is possible, if my destiny is to save the entire world or only my own. Neither seems achievable.

Sand dunes line the horizon in every direction. Wind howls. The remaining clergy form a half-circle around Renee and me. They explain that because it's a three-day journey to the next portal and heaven, our only option is to return to the monastery and face the evil.

"There are souls there left to free," says an older, bronze-skinned, ponytailed woman. "We must try. We can get to heaven from there."

Renee squeezes my hand. I feel her searching for an answer I don't have. I don't want to save the world. I only want my childhood and brother back. I want my slowly surfacing memories to return and bedtime stories without devastating evil.

It dawns on me what having a soul means. It's a way of ensuring that a part of us lives on and fights the powers of death at all cost.

✝ ✝ ✝

It happens fast. We stand motionless in the church, listening for the sounds of torment. A golden idol leers at us, a ghastly demonic head with jagged teeth and pointy ears.

"The false god of Baal," whispers the one-eyed priest.

It's the oddest feeling, seeing the same people again and again, each cloned by incredible forces, each with traces of the previous person. Regardless of what this man's name might be, he would always be Sedgwick to me. I'm glad he's alive.

This is not going to be easy. People will fall despite my efforts and possibly even because of them.

The remaining priests, nuns, and monks slink through the church with guns poised, bracing themselves around the doorway where the evil presence had been. Darkness swarms in the hall beyond.

I wonder if what I'd been told was true: the souls of the woman in white and many others are safeguarded here, held captive to prevent the rapture and Armageddon. The idea is to unlock them.

"They're at risk," Renee had explained. "If they return to God, the end begins. That's why the church stored certain souls away."

My heart exalts beyond my fear. Though I don't know where James is, I hold out hope I may see him again. The thought that the woman in white somehow survived the Forest of Forgotten Dreams drives my feet.

I lug a machine gun curled in my skinny arms and watch the first of us vanish into the living shadows of the corridor.

I'd rather die than face this again, but here I am, trying to save the only woman who'd shown me her full beauty.

In the blackness of the hall, heinous, indistinguishable messages oppress. I move through enraged spirits and lose sight of the chapel doors behind me. The dark outlines of clergy creep down the hallway. I follow with my gun at the ready, my fingers teasing the trigger.

Something flutters from the cracks in the walls and attacks. I fire, lighting the passage with bullets, screaming until my throat is hoarse. The others duck and yell until I stop. My ears ring. I kick at what appears to be a dead bat at my feet.

"Now it knows we're coming," says an older nun in a disapproving tone.

I bite my lip. "Is everyone okay?"

No one responds. I have no excuse for giving away our cover.

The remaining bats flap around us. The murky outlines of the clergy turn and move on. Terror hums inside me, while I step over the carcasses of the winged rats.

The ground rumbles, and the shadows stop. The structure shakes, sending stones from the ceiling down around us.

"Stay near the center of the hall," yells someone.

We try to avoid the tumbling blocks and falling bits of rock until the quake ends. Silt rains from the rafters and a dusty cloud robs our sight. I grope as though blind, trying to find the others, navigating chunks of debris, my gun resting in my arms. I stay the course, hoping to stumble upon a nun or priest.

Phosphorescent green light appears a little farther down the passage. Splotches on the stone floor and walls radiate a path through the maze of hallways. I call to Renee. There's no response. They're gone. I want to turn around, but there's no way back.

Near one of the splotches, I see the awkward footprints of a nun. I track the patterns until they're too thin to see. The trail leads me farther down the dingy corridor. I gather my courage and walk on.

The muzzle of the machine gun sways from one wall to the next. The image of the golden idol is fixed squarely in my mind. Recent memories make me question those I can't fully recall.

I happen on a battered wooden door hanging loosely on its hinges. Inside, three clergy lie prostrate. Blood pools around the flesh and fabric of the anointed. I did not see the rest, but I glance about with a fountain of anxiety welling in my brain. Freedom may be a curse. I wouldn't have these problems if I'd stayed in my cell.

Past the victims, between rows of shelves, lies the open hatchway of a dense vault. Around its entrance oozes more of the phosphorescent, lime-green material. An acidic smell wafts in the air. I enter and glance at the deceased, who still cling to their guns with outstretched arms, their bodies perfectly arranged in a triangle.

Heart-shaped vessels with purple ribbons and red wax seals line the vault in dense rows. I snatch one up and examine the grooves in the paraffin. Each looks many lifetimes old. The container sloshes when I tilt it.

A groan followed by the blast of machine guns radiates from somewhere far off in the building.

Frantic, I wrestle with the container and tear at the seal, wondering if there are souls are inside, if this could hold the woman in white. A hush fills the air, a silence so intense it hurts. Something stings every cell of my skin. I drop the vessel, and it cracks on the floor. Green, sludge-like liquid oozes, turning brighter as it seeps, while round after round of gunfire sounds, closer than before.

I turn to flee and catch a glimpse of a form bathed in violet light. She looks strong, a robed saint, basking in the freedom of release. She stretches as though yawning after intense sleep. A maiden, I think, a soul from the times of Rome. The contours of her body slowly materialize over the lime-green sludge. Real skin forms.

The clergy burst into the vault with cries to barricade the door, but an ungodly horde presses against the hatchway, forcing the door open. An ax flies, striking the Roman woman in the forehead. Her eyes widen in shock, and she collapses to the floor.

Sedgwick scuttles to my side, yelling and shielded by the six remaining clergy, who shoot at the horrendous figures outside. He throws two vessels to the stone ground and screams, "Release them!"

The containers crack and their contents paint the floor of the vault.

A snake-like creature with legs scurries in. An aged nun wearing a war-ready expression opens fire. Brown, wormy guts splatter and discharge a rancid smell.

The horde breaches the hatchway. Grotesque slurps and shrieks overwhelm me as ghastly creatures mount each other to invade.

Sedgwick and I slam the vessels against the floor, four and five at a time, until acid sears my flesh, and I'm deaf to the chaos. We cover our faces, but the lime-green light begs to be seen. It bends its way through our clenched eyes, until the only thing I know is intoxicating brilliance.

My senses resume with a constant explosion. I think of our dwindling ammunition. When I open my eyes, many souls of the dead stand around us, interweaved between violet luminance and flesh and blood. They seem calm amidst the thunder of guns and onslaught of evil.

A vast, dark surge of wolf, spider, and snake creatures tear into the room and pounce. We are transported by something holy, but it fails. The soulless are left behind, pinned to the monastery floor before the transfiguring rush of air.

Past the swirling waves of rainbow light, Renee and Sedgwick are shredded by evil. They shriek and reach toward us as we suddenly disappear.

Jesus's greatest miracle was the healing of people's souls through forgiveness.

—Dionysius, *Enlightened Visions*, 624 A.D.

ANDREW VI

Everything is lovely, structured, resplendent, overwhelming. A cloudless day near lapping water, satisfying, cradled in peace, a thicket of luxury, very, very old and new to the breath, meek to the extent of breaking but impenetrably strong castles in the sky made by ancient beings, groves smelling of honey, inner-warming seas, willing love, and nature without regret.

The souls survive. I watch as they observe our new surroundings with wonder. They appear both ancient and modern, with an array of features and dress: saris, kimonos, suits, ruffles, and hats, with statures ranging from childlike to giant. They run the gamut of ethnicities, physiques, and faces—fleshy and full to thin and bony.

Amidst the crowd, the woman in white blazes, a prized jewel—the kind kingdoms are fought for and lost over.

I am free, and where I wish to be at last.

But evil advances.

Deafening wails clench the joyous song in the air. The land, not earth with its known minerals, darkens under the shadow of an immense storm. We're on the tip of imagination's tongue, feeling the cold wind of mortality mount in the air around us. Wheatgrass stretches to the horizon beneath banshee moans. A sturdy, white-planked farmhouse rests on the middle of three distant hills.

I look for Renee and Sedgwick, trying to deny I'd seen them destroyed, along with many others. Only the souls from the vessels remain, each disguised with worried expressions. The woman in white peeks at me from over their shoulders— tiptoeing as she'd done in the forest.

Her eyes emote peace. "The Creator resides there."

"You mean God?" I ask. "Where?"

She points to the placid farmhouse.

"God lives on a farm?" I ask.

"That's the inner sanctum," she says. "The place God lives, our only hope."

We tread the silky blades in haste. Behind us, above us, all around us supernatural darkness brews, freezing the animated sky. Great tornados birth from the firmament, turning the land upside down, demolishing everything in their paths. As we grew near, the farmhouse resembles the home of my youth. I frantically climb onto the porch and check the door's handle. It's locked.

A clump of dirt nearby spirals high into the sky, sucking up wheatgrass and turf with the whine of a devastating machine.

The souls glance every which way. A man wearing sackcloth and a bushy gray beard exhales a mournful Latin phrase.

Renee confided in me once when we were alone: "When the rapture begins, individual life recedes, personal identity is lost, and souls return to their Creator." She'd explained the mission: "Find the birthplace of your soul and return God to the world."

I have no idea what any of this means, only that a fate worse than death awaits us if I fail.

I strike the farmhouse door with my shoulder, but I'm frail from my ordeal and the wood doesn't budge. The crowd of souls parts, as I search for a rock near the base of the porch stairs.

The ground, solid at times, morphs into the essence of spirit. I find no stone to shatter the window at the front of the house, so I kick the pane. It doesn't break. It isn't glass at all.

"How do we get inside?" I ask.

The souls speak in different languages and point toward the whirlwinds in the sky. The woman in white emerges from a sea of frightened faces. She's pure wildflowers fashioned into female curves. Blond curls bounce around her youthful face. She tunnels deep into me with her bright blue gaze.

Bits of earth drag into flight around us, stirred by the moaning tempest.

She holds out her arms as though in flight and says, "Let go."

And like that, she's sucked into the milky black ocean of clouds above us, her white dress fluttering behind her—the tail of a great, beautiful kite.

I was next. My heart lifts within me, and my core quivers with trepidation. My body feels light. I whip up into an uncontrolled spin, dizziness instantly overcoming me. Dirt pelts my body like needle pricks, and I become my own fear, curling into a ball, gritting my teeth, and trying to control my flight.

I dare to peek and see the tiny farmhouse far below and a cascade of souls accelerating toward the mouth of the funnel above. Our bodies fly against a wall of air, turning round and round.

I know the twister will heave us to the miserable ground. I search for direction and spot the woman in white, her hand stretching for mine.

We plummet, suddenly abandoned by the wind. Unspoken prayers dart through my mind.

In an instant, we're stuck in the shifting surface of this hilly world. The woman in white shrieks, while the others land, nails hammered into the ground around us. My embedded arm and leg ache. I try to leverage myself and pull them out, but can't. I sob, trapped in pain.

A soul plunges headlong into the ground nearby. He squirms, trying to dislodge himself, fighting for air. Eventually, his legs totter and collapse.

Beyond his limp body, among the tornadoes, an evil force traverses the plane. Lightning flashes in the inky sky, illuminating the wicked forms speeding toward the farmhouse.

The woman in white, stuck in the ground behind me, hooks her arm in mine and pulls full-force to free herself. She helps me out. We look over the wasteland, and tears well. Raging thunder mutes her words.

Dark creatures envelope the farmhouse like roaches on a cake. The house is imprisoned by an evil swarm. It gives way under bone-crushing weight and my heart along with it.

I avert my eyes and see the souls struggling in the ground around me. The woman in white and I help them out of the ground. I wonder if I'd failed somehow to find my way to God when I had the chance.

A morose blue tinge washes over the landscape, contrasting with the paleness of her skin. Her shoulders sink on her perfect frame. Tears fall from her cheeks. Her eyes fade into the depths of herself, watching the remains of the farmhouse being dragged apart and trampled into oblivion.

Her voice pierces the moaning wind. "Nothing's inside. No pure, blinding light, like the songs proclaim. Where's God?"

"Reliance," shouts a man with curly red hair and a battered top hat, "how are we to explain this? Is there no Creator? How can this be?"

Reliance, the woman in white, bows in a scream. "I don't know! Has evil won?"

Then I see Mastema, the man-creature from the monastery. He stands on the pulverized remains and raises his arms to the sky. Even from a distance, he glows like red-hot metal.

The ancient souls engage us with questioning stares. After being protected for many centuries, life's excavated new mysteries for them.

The wind dies and the atmosphere grows stale. The souls' faces tighten in fear. I question a future without God—a world where Saint Christopher's map leads to useless destinations.

We are truly alone. The farmhouse was the place beyond heaven where God once dwelled—perhaps millennia ago.

Reliance lies down and weeps. Her dress billows in resting air.

Why not a farmhouse? It fits with a carpenter savior and fisherman disciples. But the absence of God in its rooms slices at my faith like a sickle reaping wheat.

The man with curly red hair points and shrieks, "Run!"

The black horde draws near, a tidal wave of skeletal horses, grotesquely large wolves. Writhing beasts surge across the plane.

We plunge ahead, missing our footing, twisting ankles in consuming shadows. Green fields wilt brown before us. Flowers crumple in the valleys.

Fear flares bright, sparked by the flint and steel of my own mind. I try to escape inside, burrowing beyond the death of James to a childhood Christmas vision: laying in bed, our father reading to his twins about God's mighty works. The story of Saint Christopher was our favorite—the way he'd carry children across violent waters, an ordinary man called upon to wield mysterious power. However, all-consuming evil was left out of these stories.

Living destruction tramples the ground behind us.

I hurry, in step with Reliance, the woman in white. Her hands clutch her dress. Her feet beat a rhythm beneath her. Her face looks brilliant, even in this dying paradise.

I quickly scan the torrent of clicking claws and teeth. "Where are we going?"

She pants. "Eden."

At the summit of the next hill, we see curved garden walls in the distance, vast as a city; the lush vegetation inside remains intact though the surrounding land withers.

In the heart of the garden stands a gargantuan tree. Its top branches brush the billowing, slate-gray clouds.

Many souls flee down the hillside before us, yelling and heading for the garden's gate, as the battle-ready nightmare rattles at our backs.

We run with all the life in us, not daring to turn. Souls are slashed and slaughtered like baying cattle before a feast. Innocent blood is consumed at our heels. Ancient, warm blood sprays.

I meet Reliance's disarming eyes, for an instant, and nearly slip into the jaws of monsters.

The gate's wooden beams crash to the ground as we enter, squashing two enormous millipede-like beasts. I shudder and retreat from the sight of wild black tongues flapping along serrated teeth. Their numerous multi-jointed legs extend, searching for prey.

The multitude slams into the gate, clawing and shaking the wooden shafts.

I cling to Reliance and gasp. Only six of us made it. The others were shredded and eaten.

The red-haired man motions to a thin, Indian woman wearing a gold-and-blue sari, "Gita, the gate's not going to hold."

Beasts bite chunks of wood from the beams.

"We must eat of the tree," Gita exclaims. "There's no other way."

"Eat of the tree?" I ask.

Several souls point toward the middle of the garden, where colossal branches extend in jagged paths overhead. Bundles of vibrant yellow fruit are nestled in the tufts of pine-like needles.

The youngest man among us, dressed in modern street clothes, plucks a ripe piece. As the fruit is distributed, I remember the stories my father told about Eden and the snake.

The first of the great black wolves squeezes its way through the gate and speeds toward us. My teeth slide past the waxy coating and the sweet nectar of knowing touches my tongue.

✝ ✝ ✝

I drift sideways through the vast and deep waters of time to find the place I belong. We wake among playing children, joyous yells, boys and girls on swings racing high into the air, trying to gain on each other, to be the first to the top. A game of tag played around monkey bars and mothers rocking strollers, tending to the needs of their young. If only I could join them and reclaim all I'd lost.

I look for the others, amazed at my ability to survive. The odd-looking group was strewn throughout the park. They get to their feet under the cloudless, blue sky. The six of us who remain meet under a pavilion, relieved, mournful, and disturbed.

Reliance hacks in a bush, holding back her radiant hair. She rejoins the group, wiping her mouth. "What now?"

I turn to their hopeful, yet reluctant faces for the answer. They stare back.

"Where are we?" I ask.

The man with curly red hair brushes the dirt from his beige trousers. "This is what you'd call the real world—"

"And what we'd call the fallen world," says Gita, the woman in the sari.

I watch the children scramble for a place in line at a red slide, yipping in glee. After the storm, this seems the most peaceful place on earth.

"Are we safe?" I ask. "Can we finally stop running?"

The souls look at each other grimly.

"You must lead us," Reliance says. "They're lost in their selves of long ago, when they chose to be bottled up."

The others nod in unison, as though it'd been agreed upon.

My safe and restful feelings melt. "I know less about what's happening than anyone."

Reliance's shoulders sink. "We've all given of ourselves to stop the rapture until the church completes its work. We were kept from returning to God for that purpose."

"It's been foretold," says Gita.

"The Witnesses will open eternal doors," Reliance says. "We're not like you. You can change and follow your heart."

"We have an end in who we are," explains the man with red hair.

I shake my head.

"When you died," explains Gita, "your soul was kept from returning to The Creator by your brother."

"Because you share the same soul," says the man with red hair.

"The church kept us bottled to prevent the rapture," Reliance says.

"The end of time," says the man with red hair.

I glance at the playing children and long to join them. "But, I feel like nothing more than a child. I was robbed of my life."

They look at each other. "'And a child shall lead them,'" says Gita, triumphantly. "You must witness God."

I hide my face in my hands. "I can't."

"Then we're doomed," says the man with red hair. "Evil will be here soon and nothing will remain!"

"Stop it!" Reliance shouts. "Andrew *will* lead. He *will* witness."

I sit, sullen, on a nearby bench. "I don't know how."

Reliance draws close. Our mouths nearly touch. I taste her sweet breath as she speaks. "What does your heart tell you?"

"It's useless," says the man with red hair.

The souls walk away.

"What shall we do?" Gita asks.

I hear Reliance's voice as though in my mind. "What does your heart tell you?"

"I want to be a child again and play," I say.

"And then what? We've eaten from the fruit, Andrew. Our innocence is gone." The music of her words reaches into me and woos decision.

"I want my brother back," I cry. "I want to live." Each falling tear is stream of identity. "And, I don't want to be alone." My eyes meet hers.

She smiles like an angel discovering hope.

Gita sells her earrings at a pawnshop for enough money to buy six bus tickets to River Edge, New Jersey. I'm going home.

We eat and sleep while traveling. Honey-colored light from streetlamps pans through the bus. I fade in and out of consciousness. Reliance sits in the window seat beside me and stares out at the road as we pass through nameless towns.

"Aren't you going to sleep?" I ask.

"I've slept for so long," she says. "We all have." She looks to the others. They all stare blankly, as though in trances, not quite asleep or awake.

Even in the passing golden light, I can see her eyes are sad. "How can it be up to us to stop evil? How can we possibly keep running from those monsters?"

"It's up to you," she says, as though the words are enough.

"But why?"

"It is not for us to question the will of The Creator."

"Why did you appear on the edge of the forest when Sedgwick came to rescue me?"

Her smile is laced with sorrow. "You called to me."

"I didn't."

"The hope within you cried to the heavens. It was your hope that rescued you and awakened me, your soul."

"But the farmhouse," I whisper, afraid of the answer. "Isn't that where God lived?"

She graces me with her touch and leans close to my ear. "God lives in you."

Her words build towers of strength within me.

The bus slows to a stop. Down the aisle through headlight glare on the windshield, I see a car blocking the road.

The bus driver, a heavyset black man in a navy-blue uniform, opens the door. "What's the problem?"

Reliance squeezes my arm, her hands ice cold.

The bulky figure I know from a lifetime of nightmares enters the bus. I recognize his silhouette: Tremol.

The driver tries to stand and is pushed down. Passengers gasp. The driver tries again and is struck on the head. He crumples over and wheezes.

Tremol turns and faces the dark rows. "Now where are 'em gophers?"

Being human is knowing you have a future.

—Unknown

~ EIGHT ~

JAMES IV

Urine permeated the air.

A brunette's amber pump kicked my hand. She looked behind her, extended a half-hearted apology, and followed the crowd to the arriving train. I lay on the grime of a subway station floor amid a line of homeless, each shaking a cup with loose change.

Pain radiated from my stomach and head. I wrestled with the buttons on my shirt and discovered a stitched wound, thread holding my flesh together. Horror raced through me. I couldn't imagine what I'd done to myself.

"Get a job," slobbered an overweight man in a beige sport coat toddling to the departing train.

"I'm hurt." I screamed.

Passengers on the platform glanced in my direction, but quickly looked away. The eyes of the homeless conveyed the message of their own injuries. My forehead found refuge in my trembling palms. I'd never been so disoriented.

Seated next to me, a black man with a crusty, silver beard and a peach bandanna leaned in my direction. "You all right?"

"I just had the worst nightmare. Where am I?"

He motioned shakily toward a sign that read: "Grand Central, 42 Street, Lexington Avenue."

I blinked in remembrance. I was only two blocks from my Advertising Specialist job. Unexpectedly, work seemed like the safest place in the world.

I hobbled up concrete steps, longing for the familiarity of the city: honking taxis, boisterous bratwurst venders, flags flying over the Radisson. My head was spinning.

Instead of daylight, churning albino clouds blanketed the sky. Pedestrians filed through the streets in haste, hunkered, crossing their arms to combat howling wind. Mirrored windows reflected the swirling chaos above.

I swam through a stream of panicked New Yorkers to a skyscraper a block away. In the lobby, workers lined the front windows, searching the skyline. Others gathered around two mounted televisions and watched the local news.

"We're tracking several tornadoes in the city." The newscaster tapped a stack of papers on his desk. "Officials are telling the public to stay inside on the ground floor or in a basement and to keep away from windows. We're getting word that many buildings in Manhattan are already damaged."

A map with arrows showed the tornadoes' projected trajectories.

"This is unprecedented," the newscaster said. "Are buildings in New York designed to withstand winds of this magnitude?"

Steel doors closed and the elevator hummed to the twenty-second floor. Light jazz contrasted the storm outside. It was oddly comforting seeing not only my world, but the entire world had turned on its head.

I leaned against a wall, held the wound on my stomach, and meditated on my reflection in the elevator's blurry steel. I always thought rock bottom would be different. Whatever hallucinogen I'd unknowingly taken, they should really get it off the streets. I concocted my story: I'd been robbed and left for dead.

At first, the office upstairs appeared empty. Then, past rows of cubicles, I saw my coworkers huddled together, peering out the window. Outside, a tornado battered through a corridor of lofty buildings. My legs quivered and threatened to cave.

Mike Sanders waved and helped me to a leather sofa. His necktie strangled. His face was as red as his hair. "Are you all right?"

"I don't know," I admitted, sinking into the cushions.

"I've been waiting for you," he said.

"Why?"

Mike looked over his shoulder to make sure no one could hear. "They told me to."

"Who? Maxi?"

He smiled, searching my face. "The Order . . . of the Multiples."

I pressed my hand to my stomach to subdue a wave of nausea. "I don't know what that is."

The office staff watched the sky as though it were the movie of the week.

Mike leaned in. "What do you remember?"

My memory seized like an engine without oil. "I was mugged. Left for dead."

Maxi swept in from around a corner, clutching several magazines. "Nice of you to drop by. As soon as it's safe to leave, you can go ahead and do that. Your last check's in the mail." She snorted like a swine and led a parade of assistants into her office.

I hit the couch cushion. "Damn it!"

Mike looked past the tinted windows to an approaching funnel cloud. "Don't worry about it. It's the end of the world, and they don't even know. We need to go."

I squeezed my eyes shut. "Where? The news said not to be in the streets."

He grabbed me by the shoulder and tried to hoist me to my feet.

I freed my arm. "I'm not going anywhere. There are goddamn tornadoes out there."

Mike shook me. "Trust me."

"I don't even know you."

He pointed at my stomach. "I know that's a sacrificial wound."

"What are you talking about?" Suddenly, I felt naked in a crowd.

"You don't remember?"

I gripped the side of the couch and wondered if what I remembered could actually be real. I had nothing else. No job. No hope. Only regret for a past I barely believed.

"I think I'm losing my mind," I whispered. I wondered if Danny's Bar was open a block away.

"You're saner now than you've ever been," Mike said. "The storm's getting worse. We don't have long."

Memories crept from where I'd lost them in the bogs of drugs and alcohol. They slogged through the marshy past, searching for yesterday's painted blue skies. Brush strokes repeated until I realized the landscape of my childhood, the image of a child running after butterflies of a future. Then from the edges crept the horror: pig-faced killers, nuns birthing insects, my slain brother, alive.

I was astonished Mike might have an explanation. "I can't believe this is happening. Do you know if my brother Andrew's alive?"

Thunder clapped, rain swept over the windows.

"He'd better be," said Mike.

"That was really him? All of that stuff was *real?*"

Mike turned to the ever-darkening sky outside the window. "What's *real?* You think this is *real?*"

I nodded, absentmindedly. The wind rattled the large panes and the group retreated a step.

"Well, you may be right," Mike said. "I was told you've seen Mastema. Is evil *real?*"

A shudder ran the length of my spine. Gooseflesh pricked at my arms. "If Andrew's out there I need to find him."

Mike pulled me to my feet. "We both do. There's not much time."

The final point is not to slumber in the night of chaos: "Not to stay there, not to become beast or primeval matter but to start in a fresh direction, to discover new springs of development and action deep down in the roots of our being."

—N. J. Girardot, *Myth and Meaning in Early Daoism*, 1983

A soul is made perfect when one has traveled through all regrets to arrive at a place of regretting nothing.

—Heron of Alantical, *The Prophetic Multiple*, 140 A.D.

~ NINE ~

ANDREW VII

Tremol lumbers down the aisle of the bus.

Reliance whispers an inch from my ear. "Imagine what your life could have been. Otherwise, we all die."

I don't understand. Fear erases my thoughts. Tremol's ominous form moves through the darkness, checking rows—getting closer.

Passengers whimper, cowering in their seats, eyeing Tremol's shotgun.

Reliance's words race laps in my mind: *What your life could have been.* Images and emotions flash hints at an unclaimed life. Regrets blossom as I long for untapped possibilities.

Moments into my mantra, Arrot pleads for help outside the bus, and I see a hundred figures through the hazy windshield. Some walk before the headlights of the car and block the light. A few enter the bus.

I shiver with recognition. They look like me.

The passengers scream.

Tremol aims and fires. The blast lights up the dark bus. The chest of the first lookalike explodes, hurling him to the floor. The next in line steps past him. They keep coming.

Tremol backs up and pumps the shotgun. He's beside us. We crouch in our seats. A shot booms. Another soulless possibility falls, bloody, his flesh shredded.

I cringe, watching myself die again and again.

Shots ring outside, above Arrot's raspy shrieks.

A mob of lookalikes climb onto the bus as gunfire and cries warp the air.

They overwhelm Tremol, crowding him into submission, punching and kicking, thumping his fat until he lies motionless.

The lookalikes face me in unison, as though rehearsed. My guts churn at the sight. I look at my slack-jawed tormentor sprawled awkwardly on the floor and I weep. A wave of nausea floods my body. Freedom's empty promise gnaws at my resolve.

For decades I'd dreamt of this moment, but there's nothing sweet about Tremol and Arrot's death. I question whether they'll live on in some arcane world of memory.

Many passengers flee toward distant town lights, while a few remain inside and around the perimeter of the bus, their faces glazed with shock.

Outside, a refreshing night breeze carries a hint of rain. A group of lookalikes encompass us in the path of headlights. Arrot's lifeblood stains the road around his cracked skull.

"Do you have a soul?" asks a lookalike.

Like the others, he has russet hair, high cheeks and a broad chin. He wears the same jeans and T-shirt given to me at the monastery. Something in his fawn eyes scares me. I look to Reliance for direction. I wonder what he is. Some choice I didn't make correctly or something profoundly wrong?

He takes Reliance's hand in his own. "You are her, the most beautiful in all worlds."

Reliance blushes. "I'm only a soul."

"A soul being made perfect by The Creator," says the possibility. "Wonderful, wonderful. I'm Carter." He draws her hand to his chest. "Never did I think I'd have such a chance at life." He raises his fist. "We must fight evil at all cost to save the mortal world and protect the souls!"

The souls gather from the bus and fields, along with a thousand possibilities to hear his words.

The few hysterical passengers who remain flee into the night. They scatter down the road and try to hitch a ride from the cars meandering through the scene. Late-night drivers slow seeing the bus and mob. They speed off after a closer look.

Carter climbs onto the hood of Tremol and Arrot's car and points to the lightning flashing in the East. "Evil is coming! We must plan an attack!"

Reliance and the others are drawn by his words. Carter is not a failure I realize, but rather a success I may have forfeited or have yet to experience in life.

I stand by Reliance's side as Carter rallies his troops. I know that should be me up there, enacting desire, but the stakes are lost on me, the alternatives so much stronger. Our attempts to confront evil in the past failed so miserably, I see no way out.

Carter addresses the remaining souls nestled in a crowd of alternative me's, "What has God decided?"

"We are following the twin," yells the red-haired man with the battered top hat. "He may be one of the Witnesses."

"His heart will lead the way," adds Gita.

Carter's eyes narrow. "As you know, I am only a soulless possibility, praise be to God. But I ask you, is following the heart of a man the smartest thing? 'The heart is deceitful and desperately wicked.'"

A hush falls on the crowd. Far off the sky peals with thunder.

"Where's God?" asks someone.

"There aren't enough of us to fight evil," shouts another.

"Let's run," another says. "We can hide the souls where they'll never be found."

My resolve melts. I look up at Carter. "What would you have us do?"

The remaining souls burn me with their stares, their expressions sour and distant.

"One of the soulless cannot lead us," pleads the woman with the silver ponytail.

"We must fight!" Carter shouts. "This is one of the last worlds. Once evil is at home here, nothing will remain!"

"Where is following the twin getting us?" sounds a voice from the crowd.

"I never claimed to be a leader!" I scream.

A thousand accusatory murmurs ensue.

I throw my hands in the air. "I never asked anyone to follow me. You want to follow Carter, follow Carter."

He accepts his inauguration with a grin.

"No," Reliance shouts, "it is written: 'Two sharing a soul shall usher God into the world.'"

A storm mounts in the East, spreading through the sky with billowing clouds. I flee. The masses of identical men part to make a path. Their eyes follow my steps, until I am alone, along the road, seeking solace in the unformed expectations of tomorrow. Gravel crunches underfoot. The wind strengthens. I wonder what one can hope to achieve after witnessing the death of God.

I open the door and a bell jingles. Inside, hamburger grease saturates the air, decorative pies rotate in a display case at the counter. Many passengers from the bus occupy booths. Every eye meets mine.

Susie, the taller of two well-endowed waitresses, dressed in baby-blue uniforms, stirs chocolate syrup into a glass of milk and sets it in front of a mustached, middle-aged man sitting at the counter. Next to him, a bleached blond strains her vowels. "I just couldn't believe it. We barely escaped with our lives!"

She turns, sees me, and grows silent. Only the clink of dishes from the kitchen and the hum of the revolving pie tray can be heard.

"Anywhere, hon," Susie says, her name printed in large letters on a tag clipped to her uniform.

There's one booth open in the far corner where an elderly couple is leaving. I slide in, glance at the menu, and try to interpret what people are mumbling. My mind toys with fragments of a new reality. The time I'd spent locked up and wishing for escape seems lifetimes ago.

"The special's halibut with a vegetable medley." Susie's gum threatens to leap from her mouth onto the table. "You on that bus, too? They say there was some sort of shooting?"

Everyone watches me.

I nod. "Sounds fine. I'll have that."

"Looks like you could use a slice of lemon meringue pie." Susie taps my bony shoulder with her pen.

Some patrons leave the diner, shooting glances over their shoulders. Others return to their meals, keeping one eye on me.

The silver bus rolls into view in front and stops with a belch of compressed air. Splattered blood frosts its rear windows.

Scores of identical men turn their heads and peer out of the bus in unison. A restless wave passes through the restaurant.

A muffin tumbles off a plate in Susie's hand. A cup of coffee slides off a table and crashes on the floor.

The remaining patrons clear out at breakneck speed, leaving only a few stunned people behind.

The bus doors open and Reliance descends; her pure white dress cascading the steps. She strolls into the diner and sits next to me as the bus drives off into the night. While I'm overjoyed to see her, I'm also aware she carries massive responsibility.

Her pale skin glows radiant under the neon lights. Her bouncy blond curls play on her shoulders.

"Where are they going?" I ask.

"To fight evil."

"What can they possibly do?"

She brushes the hair from her face with her tender hand. "They will do what they can."

"Where are the others?"

"Walking."

Thousands of men who look like me walk toward a distant evil storm. I feel I should be among them, but I don't move.

Reliance takes a menu from the table. "What's good?"

"Why are you here?" I ask.

"My place is with you."

I look around the deserted diner. "I've got nowhere to go."

"You've got to follow your heart to where I was born."

"I thought my heart was wicked."

"It is," she says, "but it's the only heart we've got."

"You know, when I saw you on the edge of the forest, I thought you were the answer to all my problems. I thought if I could simply be with you, freedom would have meaning.

"I dreamt of killing those two bastards my entire life, but you know what? They're dead, and I don't feel any better. I feel worse. I'm here with you, and I don't even know what you want from me. What do you think I can possibly give you?"

Her voice softens. "It's not about what you can give me. It's about finding God."

"I thought God was dead," I say, "after the farmhouse."

She sighs. "God lives in you. You just have to find him."

Susie calls to us from the kitchen where she'd disappeared after seeing the bus full of lookalikes, "We're going to have to ask you to leave. We're closing early."

Two sheriff's cars pull up outside.

"My heart's telling me we should get out of here," I say.

Reliance takes my hand and searches my eyes.

I know I can go anywhere with her. "Why was I held captive while my brother lived his life? I lost James twice, and each time my heart was torn in two."

We look up. Two deputies stand beside our table, hands on their guns.

We have found a strange footprint on the shores of the unknown. We have devised profound theories, one after another, to account for its origins. At last, we have succeeded in reconstructing the creature that made the footprint. And lo! It is our own.

—Sir Arthur Eddington, *Space, Time, and Gravitation*, 1920

The secret of life is to "die before you die" — and find that there is no death.

—Eckhart Tolle, *The Power of Now*, 1999

~ TEN ~

JAMES V

We left the basement parking garage in Mike Sanders's coup and crept up the ramp into a downpour, rolling past the security guard reading a paperback novel. He was unaware the world was ending, unaware that we were driving out into the last storm on earth.

I looked again and the guard was far too hairy to be human. Long tufts of gray-black hair sprouted from his head and face. He turned and clawed at the booth's Plexiglas as rain swept over the car.

It was only three o'clock, but the city was washed in twilight. The figures on the sides of the road, once rushing for cover, appeared stationary, huddled in black business suits, raincoats, and beneath umbrellas. Some grasped at their own heads and necks, choking.

I pressed my face against the window. "What's happening?"

"There's nothing you can do for them," Mike said. "Without God in the world, they're turning into their true selves."

We drove slowly beside cars stopped in the middle of the road.

A beer commercial flashed inside the barred windows of an electronics shop. In front, a pig-faced man ripped at the buttons on his shirt.

Mike sped up the car.

"My God. What was that?"

Mike swerved.

The car suddenly hit a man. His head cracked the windshield, and he spun onto the ground. We lurched to a stop.

I reached for the handle.

"Don't," Mike yelled and jammed the car into reverse.

The man stood in the path of the headlights, holding his bleeding head and staggering toward us. Black scales emerged, shredding his clothes until they studded the length of him.

I braced myself. "Go!"

The tires screeched as we sped by him and turned the corner onto another street.

"What the hell is happening?"

"I told you," Mike said. "They're being shown for what they are."

"All over New York?"

"Everywhere! Everyone but multiples."

"Multiples?"

"Twins, triplets, quadruplets."

I slid down in my seat trying to disappear. "This is insane!"

"Multiples share the same soul," Mike said. "If one of them dies, their soul is no longer inside them, and they can go anywhere a soul can go."

My head ached with disbelief, rivaling the pain in my stomach.

Mike felt around under his seat. "They were supposed to teach you all of this."

I tried to stop my arms and legs from shaking. "Who?"

"Your Helpers. Preventing the rapture has an effect, just like fighting a virus with a vaccine. The virus gets stronger."

We sped by a cluster of shadowy figures on a street corner. Each held a coat over their head, protecting themselves from the rain. They tracked the car as we passed.

"We try to control evolution by treating disease, interrupting life's cycle, but nature reemerges with a vengeance." Mike turned down two more streets. "The physical and spiritual are the same. Things mutate. Evil evolves."

We slowed at a line of unnaturally large figures blocking the road. Steam rose from manhole covers. Fur protruded from torn clothes. Two enormous centipedes scurried into sight.

Mike looked behind us. "Shit."

Creatures were there, too, closing in.

He pointed. "Get the gun out of the glove box."

I froze, suddenly a terrified eight year old.

"Get it out or we're going to die." He reached over and fumbled with the latch.

The figures approached, shielding their eyes from the headlights: men with the heads of boars and gigantic black wolves in tattered clothing.

The gun dropped to the floor between my legs.

"Pick it up," screamed Mike.

I hesitated, my arms limp with fear.

Tires spun as Mike forced the gas pedal and reached for the Glock. The coup veered forward and hit a wolf. He clutched at chrome and howled. We veered back and forth, trying for the street. We crashed into a fire hydrant. The wolf clawed at the hood trying to tear himself free.

A pigman stood outside my window. The fleshy pink of his face shone under a streetlight. Mike was out cold, his head tilted on the headrest.

The pigman rammed the window with his shoulder. Glass spider-webbed.

I searched the floorboard and found the cool steel of the semi-automatic. The pigman crashed in.

I aimed and squeezed the trigger. Nothing happened. Bloody arms swung wildly and the pigman grabbed my neck. I pushed my feet against the door, trying to get free, but his hold tightened. He snorted among a chorus of excited squeals.

I ran my fingers down the side of the gun, flipped off the safety, and squeezed the trigger.

A shot exploded.

The windshield shattered.

The pigman yanked hard, slamming my face into the dash. I aimed and fired. Hot blood splattered. His gnarly hands loosened.

A centipede rattled onto the hood, crushing the front of the car with its weight. Its scissor-like jaws opened and closed as it forced its way through the windshield.

Alien eyes sought me out. Its mouth snapped inches from where my body was pinned against the seat.

I fired and hit the dash—stunned deaf. The gun dropped to the floor from the cracking recoil.

A thousand needlelike teeth bit into my shoulder and tried to shovel me in.

I wailed for help. My fingertips stabbed for the gun, but it was out of reach.

The transmission jolted. The car skidded in reverse. Mike was awake. He steered, swaying in his seat, trying to drive. We built momentum despite the centipede's weight and eventually slid out from under the giant insect.

The car pummeled a horde of dark creatures. They leapt at the open windows. Mike shrieked and shifted gears. The coup lurched forward, trying to gain speed amid the freakish crowd.

We drove on, dragging the carcass of a wolf and a pigman, the car's crushed side groaning against the tire. We stopped after two blocks. Steam hissed from the radiator.

Mike held his head to stop a trickle of blood. "Get out. We're going to have to run for it."

"Where?"

Shadows lurked against the dim exteriors of buildings and walkways. Snorts and grunts echoed in alleys. All around us, the nightmare multiplied.

We ran. Mike held his leg. I tried to distance the pain of my shoulder and stomach. We climbed a fire escape ladder past a second-floor apartment and into a third. Mike stumbled into the bedroom and bathroom, holding the gun out, checking for beasts.

The drab apartment had an off-white linoleum floor, peeling polka-dotted wallpaper, and Ansel Adams prints in plastic frames. I collapsed on a sofa.

The sounds of Hades swirled through the window from the alley below. Something alive was being torn apart. I was thankful it wasn't us.

The deadbolt on the door appeared latched, but the misery of my shoulder and stomach kept me from checking. I eyed a bottle of vodka on the kitchen counter. It seemed lifetimes away. For the first time I could remember, I didn't want it.

Mike slid the gun onto the table and sat down. He blotted at the blood running down his forehead with his necktie.

I felt for the reassuring stitches on my stomach. "We never should have left the office!"

Mike spun the semi-automatic like a dreidel on the table. "There's nothing to go back to. They're all monsters."

Tears welled in my eyes. "What do we do now? Wait for them to come up here and kill us?"

Mike loaded another clip with bullets he pulled from the pockets of this slacks. "The Order said you'd know what to do."

"Me? How the hell would I know what to do? The entire world's upside down."

"I'm supposed to take you to where your soul was born. That's my job. You weren't told anything?"

"No, I wasn't told anything! What do you mean 'the place my soul was born'?"

Mike ran his hands through his hair and stared off into space. "You must know."

"No one told me anything! I don't want to die."

A faint scraping sound grew louder, until it stopped outside the door.

We exchanged glances.

Mike reached for the gun and held it in his shaky hands. "How can you not know where your soul was born?"

"I never even thought I had a soul."

Mike clenched his eyes shut. "An unbeliever? How were you even chosen?"

"I wasn't chosen. I'm in advertising."

The door handle rattled.

Mike motioned for me to join him at the table.

I couldn't move. The grunts and snorts in the alley below leapt to octaves of malicious hilarity.

The handle stopped rattling.

"Get over here now," said Mike.

A specter flashed past the open bedroom door, flitting in the corner of my eye. At first I thought I'd imagined it. Then, I noticed movement in the dim room. I tried to swallow the lump forming in my throat.

I found the strength to join Mike at the table.

The front door crashed open and Mike fired. It was a man who looked just like him, two or three of them. The one in front took the bullet. He leaned forward, held his stomach, and collapsed to the floor. The others gathered around and tried to help.

Mike nearly collapsed. "I'm sorry. I didn't know."

Other possibilities appeared from the bedroom, rushing to the injured man's side.

Mike looked me in the eyes. "My God, I've been trained for this. Not now!"

The lookalikes turned the fallen man onto his back and placed a towel under his head. His black cotton dress shirt was open, showing a hole where the bullet entered.

Andrew's death, all those years ago, attacked me like demons from the sky.

Mike kneeled and took the man by the arm. "Who are you? Who were you supposed to be?"

The man coughed on his own blood.

The others pushed Mike away and said, "Leave him alone. Let him die in peace."

Mike backed off. "I'm sorry. I'm so sorry."

I saw myself in Mike, remembering standing over Andrew's motionless form. There wasn't enough regret in the entire world to give the moment justice.

Too many to count, the lookalikes spoke all at once about different things.

"They're all me," Mike said. "I just killed part of myself. What if that guy was a loving father?"

I noticed the hellish sounds outside had stopped. "We should get out of here."

Mike squeezed the bridge of his nose and nodded. "You have to return to where your soul was born. Then you can face what you must in order to bring God back into the world."

"Face what?"

"'Twins once dead shall rise again', it's prophesied."

"No idea what you're talking about."

"Don't you know the prophecies about the Witnesses?"

"No!"

"The last remaining twins will be the vessels that bring God back into the world."

My legs no longer held me. I sat on the floor, stunned, surrounded by chatting Mike Sanders lookalikes. I used to joke with this guy in the lunchroom at work, and now he's telling me it's up to me to save the world.

"It's my job to get you there," said Mike.

I slapped myself in the face. "This can't be real. Any minute I'm going to wake up."

Low, fierce growls sounded in the hall and alley, escalating to aggression.

"They're dying," Mike screamed. "My future is dying."

I watched as he took the gun and charged the door.

We have a primal and therefore a higher self.

—Samuel Grim

Emotion + Consciousness = The Soul

—Christopher Hawke

~ ELEVEN ~

ANDREW VIII

Diner tables sit empty. Susie and the other staff peek at Reliance and me from the safety of the kitchen. I sense the ignorance simmering behind the deputies' regulated dispositions.

"I.D. please," says the thin one.

"I ate at a place like this with my parents when I was a child," I say.

Reliance sits up straight and looks them both in the face. "A great evil has come into the world."

The beefier one motions for us to get up. "And we want you to tell us all about it."

"At the station. Come on." The other officer takes Reliance by the elbow.

They pat us down and put us in the back of separate squad cars. We head toward the highway. The deputy speaks jargon into the radio about bringing us to the station. Reliance peers through the back window of the car in front.

Distant lights glitter from towns on the other side of farmland. The night seems final, the end of something wonderful.

"They're looking for a bus," the deputy says, meeting my eyes in the rearview mirror. "Where were you headed?"

"River Edge, New Jersey," I say. "The others were taking me there."

"What others?"

"The souls from the monastery."

He doesn't say anything else for some time. Then he asks, "Why were you going to Jersey?"

"I think it has something to do with my brother killing me when I was eight," I say.

"Killing you?"

I nod.

"You mean hurting you?" he asks.

"No. I'm starting to believe I was dead. I still might be for all I know."

He pauses. "Have you ever been in an institution?"

"I've hardly been in school at all. I think I know some things because I share a soul with my twin."

He sighs deeply and focuses on the road.

I know I must sound crazy, but I can only keep one reality in my head at a time. Most of my life, I'd lived as a caged animal. Regardless of what I do today or where I am I can't escape from that. Something inside tells me I shouldn't try. The point of life is building my own self, an identity of my own. In an inexplicable way, the storm on the horizon spurs my belief that the world of my youth, lost for so long, is of utmost importance.

Everything for these souls is fueled by mere intention: to be free, to have hope, to lead others in a fight against evil, to bring God back into the world. How can I possibly bring God back into the world, be it mine or anyone else's? I'm afraid to ask, afraid of an answer requiring brave action, afraid to explore my dark heart, and feel my flesh for a dismal pulse of hope.

The squad car veers. Tires rumble on the side of the road. The deputy regains control, covers his mouth, and hacks. The car in front swerves back and forth, flashes its brake lights, and coasts to a stop.

We skid into a field, and I'm thrown to the floor. The stench of stomach acid follows another bout of the deputy's retching. The heaving sounds like a bewildered scream morphing into a growl.

I sit up cautiously and peek over the front seat.

Rough, black fur sprouts from the deputy's flesh. His hands grab at the dash in terror and suddenly straighten with the force of electrocution. His body vibrates. Agony contorts his face. His eyes darken in painful confusion as his torn lips curl, and his mouth stretches into snapping jaws. I throw myself against the locked door again and strike the unbreakable glass with the heel of my foot.

The wolf lunges at the Plexiglas separating us, butting the side of his newly forming head until crimson streaks appear. He bellows in rage, shakes his head with its tufts of black fur, and repeatedly thrusts at the inside of the driver's side door. The handle catches, flips up, and releases him. Outside, he grapples with the rear door to get at me, his nails peeling metal. I shrink to the opposite side of the car in a futile attempt to distance myself.

Woofing like human laughter transforms into manic yelps as his scalpel-sharp nails scrape the handle.

The door cracks open.

A horn blares. Someone yells far off. Reliance waves her arms in the air next to the car in front.

The beast tears after her, running on all fours. She quickly slides beneath the car. He's there at once, shaking the vehicle.

Gathering my courage, I pray and kick the door. It flies open.

The wolf rocks the car in front higher and higher, trying to get at Reliance. Inside, a pigman rams the glass to free itself.

I rack my mind for a solution and fight the urge to run into the safety of the dark fields. I slide into the driver's seat, rev the engine, and honk the horn. The wolf turns and bares his canines.

I mash the gas petal and steer toward the beast, building speed. He leaps onto the car's roof just before impact. I spin the car around and spot Reliance hiding under the other squad car.

Glass explodes. Shards slice my face. The wolf grabs my head, rakes me though the shattered window, and hurls me to the street. I struggle to breathe and drag myself along the ground. He dives, flips me over, and pries at my chest with knife-like claws.

A shot blasts. Reliance stands nearby, armed with a smoking shotgun. The wolf throws its head from side to side. Blood spews from its mouth. I hide my face and grab at the creature's arms, trying to dislodge the nails. They sink deeper.

Reliance aims and fires again. The wolf shrieks and flees into the field.

Reliance kneels beside me. "Are you all right?"

It feels as though a searing rod scorches my chest. "What happened? Why did he become that thing?"

The beast whines in the surrounding darkness.

"That's what he always was," Reliance says. "He'll be back."

I try to stand.

She helps me to my feet. "It's time to decide if you're going to change the world."

"I don't know how."

"Time's running out. This is happening to everyone. It's up to you to bring The Creator back into the world."

My legs grow weak beneath me. My body sways, ready to topple.

"Why me? Where's God?"

From somewhere in the field, the wolf threatens with deep-throated growls. The pigman cracks his head against the other squad car's bloody Plexiglas window.

Reliance helps me to the safety of the other vehicle.

I brace myself on the steering wheel. "Why were we going to the house I died in?"

"If your heart's right you'll know. It's the place you first laughed and cried, the place where your emotions met your intellect, and I was born."

"How do I make my heart right?"

"Become a child again."

Her words fill me with understanding, knowledge I'd lost when I was eight. I engage the engine and set out for River Edge, New Jersey, led by intuition, hoping against hope I'll find James again and reclaim my lost life.

It is the experience of the human mind in its imaginative operation as itself radically ambiguous, essentially anomalous, inescapably multivalent—facing both out and in, linking above and below, animal-like and godlike, social cog and individual solitude, shaped and shaping, part of all that is but only as a subject knowing its own apartness.

—Robert D. Pelton

Faith is the strength behind words.

—Heron of Alantical, *The Prophetic Multiple*, 140 A.D.

~ TWELVE ~

JAMES VI

The hall teemed with spines and fur, pig flesh and scaly lashing legs. Mike fought alongside the crowd of red-haired lookalikes. Jarring screams and growls filled the air. I lost track of which one he was. Then he fired. The soulless Mikes were slashed and chewed by the fangs of wolves and chattering teeth of pigs. Bullets struck a few monsters, and they were quickly trampled.

Meaty sticks were among the horde, new white-veined creatures with needlelike noses and chins. They struck their forearms together and made clacking sounds that pierced my eardrums. They climbed in through the fire escape windows with jerky movements, as though animated by Satan.

We're going to die a final death. There's no God-controlled world to return to.

I grabbed a wooden chair, prepared to swing. Mike hobbled from the hall and fired at advancing stickmen until the gun clicked empty. One fell and white blood splattered onto the walls and floor.

We retreated to the bedroom and slammed the door, wedging the chair under the doorknob. Snorts, howls, and clacks grew deafening on the other side. The door rattled on its hinges. We cowered in the corner, expecting the end. But soon, the hellish racket faded to a disturbing silence.

A bedtime melody sounded from the other side. The singing voice reminded me of my father's, only not quite right, a chorus of one when it should have been many. The tune itself was from the pit of an asylum.

A knock sounded once, then again with impatience.

Mike and I eyed each other, distraught. Fear burrowed into me.

The answer flew into my mind, like a dove in a vision. I'd kept my parent's home intact many years after their deaths. There was no other comfort I could extend to the ghosts that lived there.

"I think I know where we need to go," I said.

Mike was ashen-faced, muttering parts of an inner-dialog aloud. "My future's gone. They're all dead."

The knock sounded again.

"What is that?" I murmured.

Mike stared blankly at the floor. "Mastema."

The name chilled me to the bones.

A stickman leered in one of the bedroom windows, pressing his needle-nose against the glass.

The wooden door bowed, warped inward by an unseen force. The chair under the knob scraped the floor and gave way, smacking against the wall.

Mastema, the manlike creature, birthed from the nun at the monastery, stood alone in the doorway. He was clothed in a black, Egyptian pharaoh-like garb with interwoven swirly silver threads. His hard-etched face pointed downward in a fixed, stern expression. Beasts crouched in the background, ready to attack, like dogs biting at invisible chains.

The edges of Mastema's mouth turned up as he stepped into the room. An inferno of air preceded his entrance.

He spoke with a charged voice. "Where are the others?"

Mike spit in Mastema's direction. "Don't tell him anything. He's the devil."

Mastema laughed. "You know only what you've been told." He ran his ringed index finger down the length of his cheek. "There are two sides to everything."

"Yeah," Mike said, "good and *evil*."

Mastema paced the room, the fantail of his coat brushing the linoleum floor. He squinted at the ceiling in frustration. "In the final days, men are shown for what they are. You are unchanged. Explain yourselves."

"God will stop you," said Mike.

"I am the creator," Mastema barked. "I tread on your God's ashes."

"Liar," Mike shouted.

Mastema twisted his face into mock sorrow. "It's unfortunate for you that I speak the truth. Those who fear the truth fear life."

Subdued growls and random clacks from the stickmen's arms filled the other room.

Mastema glanced at the beasts through the doorway. "See for yourselves. This is reality. Man is nothing more than animal."

"You made them that way," Mike screamed.

Mastema grinned. "I only exposed the way things are. I knocked and your *God* didn't answer. Would you rather go on believing in something that isn't true?"

"God's alive," said Mike.

Mastema stepped closer. "I am he. The *inner sanctum* was empty."

A wave of hostility coursed through the room. The creatures yowled.

"I'll give you one chance," Mastema said. "Bring the remaining humans to me, and I will let you live." His fiery stare awaited our decision. "You have already given up everything for nothing. Your future and past lie dead. I will give you a new future."

Mike averted his eyes. "Only The Creator can save us."

"Of course, and I will." Mastema stooped down and lifted my chin with his searing finger. "What do you say? This is not tomorrow or yesterday, but a world of now, forever. This world is yours if you pledge your soul to me."

Jaundiced fire burned behind the narrow slits of his eyes. I searched for an escape there, a bluffing gambler betting on more than he understood.

"I don't want the world," I said.

He forced a smile through frozen sadness and let escape his charcoal breath. "I see. Guilt is your bargain. Your conscience has enslaved you. I will free you of the mundane past if you make me your master."

"Don't listen to him," Mike pleaded.

Mastema extended his hand in Mike's direction and silenced him with invisible power, then turned to me. "What do you say? I can give you the life you've always wanted, a life free of guilt. We'll kill off your regrets one by one."

Mike slumped motionless in the corner.

I mulled over the decision. Returning inside to every Alcohol Anonymous step I'd ever done, I searched my regrets, thinking back to all the lost souls I'd encountered. I looked squarely at Andrew's death and choked back tears.

Mastema shattered the plaster on the wall with a strike of his fist. "Tell me. Do you choose life or death?"

"I want to live," I said, surprising myself with the answer.

Mike groaned in disagreement.

"Keep my friend alive and you have a deal," I said.

Mastema reached down and grasped my jaw, kneading his fingers into my flesh. "You have three days to return with the remaining humans, or I will wipe you from existence in pain beyond your imagination."

He offered me his hand, and I took it with a swallow of fate. The handshake singed my soul.

You cannot find yourself by going into the past. You can find yourself by coming into the present. Life is now. There was never a time when your life was not now, nor will there ever be.

—Eckhart Tolle, *The Power of Now*, 1999

To be a man is to feel that one's own stone contributes to building the edifice of the world.

—Antoine de Saint-Exupery

~ THIRTEEN ~

ANDREW IX

The rhyme my parents taught James and me blows through my memory, a gust of intoxicating air: *If you get lost and need to find your way back, follow Kinderkamack to the tracks. Then a left. You'll find your way home, just turn right on Howland.*

The house I grew up in looks oddly like the two-story farmhouse in heaven, an untouched corpse of a building locked away behind chain-link fence, hidden behind overgrown oaks and ivy. On either side, shiny new structures with well-manicured shrubs and lawns challenge its survival.

Paint peels from its wood siding. Plants rooted in the shingles of the roof rise to meet pockets of light piercing the oak canopy.

Memories override what my eyes see, like the aged visiting the elderly and recalling the past with such passion as to make today obsolete. The place is as I remember it, a home of God and family, like once upon a time in a fairytale.

Reliance and I duck through a bend in the chain-link gate and avoid a sign that reads: *Private Property. Keep Out.*

"James must have kept the house all these years," I say. "It used to be one of the nicer homes on the block."

As before, when we'd transported to other dimensions, this place is otherworldly and connects me to the hidden world of yesterday as nothing ever has. A familiar door reveals itself through a path lined with overgrown bushes.

"This is the same as the house in heaven," I say with wonder.

"What you see is for you to see," Reliance says. "It's what something represents that's important. To you it's a house in space and time; to someone else, it could be anything. Only the inside's important."

"What's inside?" I ask.

"Reality."

The porch creaks under my weight. I turn the bronze handle and shoulder the door open. The house exhales stale air.

Reliance stayed on the path, several paces behind.

"Aren't you coming?" I ask.

"This is for you alone," she says.

"I don't want to go by myself."

"You must."

I step inside, amidst the dust, cobwebs, and sheeted furniture. Things are as I remember: the decorative, etched mirror over the fireplace mantel, Mother's favorite tasseled lampshades, and the carved designs in the L staircase.

Ghosts that haunted me all my imprisoned years escape the confines of the past and arrive in the moment. Memories bring me to my knees.

I remember following James downstairs when I was a boy, arriving at an immense evergreen, decorated in ornaments and blinking red, green, blue, and gold. Beneath, lay the presents we'd hoped for all year—neatly wrapped in glistening paper, identical gifts for identical twins.

Our sleepy-eyed parents descend behind us, resonating warm protection. More than the hysteria of unwrapping presents, I notice the arches of love they've built above us. These structures were intended for support in our later lives. Only now, these stones lie bare and scattered like excavated ruins. One can only dream of the intent and ask what kind of lives and people such structures were designed for.

My vision takes me into our room upstairs. James and I duck behind our beds, playing shootout with our new plastic cap guns. I follow James into our parents' room. He balances on the stool in the closet and pries the lid off a box. We marvel at the glint of the steel revolver, its enormous weight in our eight-year-old hands. My brother squeezes the trigger.

I'm sure my mother rushed upstairs. I'm sure my father woke from his nap on the couch. I'm sure James held the picture in his mind's eye forever.

Tears stream. A storm of regret and pain swirl within me. Anger surfaces at the thought of all the days and nights I've lost. I know the harm. Shame fuels the negative, until hate clouds my vision, and I'm blind in the room of my youth. The thoughts of forgiveness I've harbored slip from my sight and are lost.

Someone like Reliance takes my hand. Her palm burns, a kettle on a fire. Her fingers stoke iron rods. I yank my hand away and try to soothe it.

Her face is a blur, her voice sultry and deeper than usual. "Life is not something you can be given. It's something you must take."

Everything transforms and upturns like silt at the bottom of a raging sea. When calm returns, it appeared as though I'm outside. A billion stars wink in an expanding sky. Beside me, instead of Reliance stands Mastema, the manlike creature from the monastery. I stumble back and fall to my knees.

Draped on his overwhelming frame are the historic, midnight-black clothes of a pharaoh. He stoops and places a hand on my shoulder. Heat torches through my shirt.

"You poor boy," he says. "You want only to live. Your life was stolen when you were too young to know what life was."

Powerful heat radiates from him. I imagine my head sliced from my shoulders and landing with a thud on the ground beneath me. Mastema appears ready to do worse.

"I can return your life," he says. "Take away pain and regret. Remove the loss, give you what you deserve."

I look up into his honed eyes. He resembles an enormous falcon ready to descend at light-tearing speed.

I yelp like a wild animal and cover my head.

He straightens his back and flaps the edges of his coat at his sides.

"What do you want?" I blubber.

"Only what you want," he says. "Life."

He chuckles, takes my arm, and hoists me to my feet. "Life is not what you believe it to be. It's more than you can imagine." He sweeps the side of my shoulder with his hand, picks off and flicks away a piece of lint.

"I do want life. I'm sure we're not all that different." I say this in hopes he doesn't decimate me, but my words ring true in my ears.

"It's not fair, what happened to you," Mastema says. "I will set things right."

The heavens seem reachable above us, and Mastema touches the stars with his words: "I will set all things right!"

The atmosphere sours, half-breathed. A graveyard lies before us. Walls of mist section us off from the world.

Mastema strolls through old and new tombstones and stops at a short grave. "Have you seen your marker?"

I peer at the marble slab framed in sod and find no words to answer.

He says, "You must recognize reality to comprehend what I offer."

Holding his arms before him, he curls his fingers toward the wispy-gray sky. The ground pulses in waves, overflowing, a geyser of black dirt, sand, and clay. The marble cracks and turns over in pieces. Dirt covers the headstone and piles around us. We grow small among the mounds, until the upheaval stops and hardened dirt stairs lead to a small unearthed casket.

My heart spasms. I scream—on fire.

The casket lid flies off and drops beside us with a thud. The thin cloth covering the corpse's face flutters in the back draft. The Sunday suit I'd worn to church on Easter mornings limply supports the bones.

Mastema grins.

A gush of wind lifts the cloth, flapping skyward, a wedding dove escaping a cage. A child's shattered skull lies below.

Mastema sounds close, as though in a small room. "This is undeniable, Andrew."

I fall and crawl, grasping handfuls of soil in an attempt to distance myself from my grave. An internal monster of emotion seizes and shakes my body until my eyes flood. I hate, yet I see a new future of my very own. Claiming uncharted land like an explorer, I shake Mastema's hand and agree to everything.

A map's purpose is to filter out chaos.

—Dionysius, *Enlightened Visions*, 624 A.D.

~ FOURTEEN ~

JAMES VII

As Mike Sanders drove, the stickman jittered in my peripheral sight, watching us from the backseat, his eyes darting back and forth. My shoulder and stomach simmered with pain, but they seemed trivial compared to the weight of my agreement with Mastema.

Under different circumstances, my newfound sobriety would have proved a great achievement, but it seemed hardly worth noting with the world ending.

Mike glanced at the creature in the rearview mirror, then at me. "I'm not taking you to find anyone."

I edged toward the door. "Can that thing understand us?"

"I don't know," said Mike.

The stickman whistled gently with each breath.

"What the hell is it?"

Mike sped up. "Something horrible. Everything's upside down, if you hadn't realized."

"I noticed." I didn't know what my agreement meant, but it had saved our lives—for now. The thought of "pain beyond imagination" made me thirsty for after work happy hour. "Where are we going?"

"Out of the city, where you're sure not to find any other humans."

I leaned in. "Listen, Mike—"

He pointed my direction. "I'd keep my distance if I were you."

"You don't understand. I only said those things to get us out of there alive."

Mike groaned, studying my face for truth. "You made an agreement with evil. Didn't you realize what you were doing?"

"No," I screamed. "I was saving our lives."

The stickman clacked his arms together. Mike and I yelled at it to shut up.

The creature looked dumbfounded, ready to club us to bloody pulps. Fortunately, somewhere in the recesses of its warped skull it clung to obedience.

I wondered how I knew this, if it was because I too was snared, awaiting a command. "Isn't there somewhere we can hide?"

Mike didn't answer. He fixated on the road, weaving through abandoned and crashed vehicles. I envied him having something to concentrate on other than the wheezing monster we chauffeured.

Towns full of the devolving coped with their misfortune in shredded suits and dresses, watching as we drove past, like serpents enticed by a fleeing mouse.

I ran my fingers along the stitches on my stomach. "We can't possibly fight this."

Mike peered back at the creature, then at me.

I glanced at the stickman. It stared back and made a whistling noise, looking nearly human in the way it tilted its thin head and puckered its white lips.

"The Order came to me and my sisters when we were just out of college," Mike said. "They claimed there were other worlds we could be part of because we were multiples, just like Jesus."

"Jesus was a multiple?"

"Of course. How else could he bridge worlds? You don't know much, do you?"

"Less all the time."

"Triplets," Mike said. "My sisters and I went to the university at the monastery and traveled to other worlds using Saint Christopher's map. Do you know the story?"

I nodded, wishing I'd paid more attention to Renee's explanation. "I was right there with Andrew, and I treated him like shit. I shot and killed him, and when I had the chance—"

"Stop. This is mind-bending stuff. It's not every day you meet your dead brother."

I swallowed the lump in my throat. "Tell me about it. If only I'd known."

"You know now. It's not too late."

We followed the ramp onto the highway, roving through where panicked drivers abandoned their cars.

I couldn't believe the end of the world was really here. "How can we travel to other worlds just using a map?"

"Because on it God revealed parts of reality that weren't yet imagined. That's the key: concepts straight from the mind of The Creator. The church realized the significance of multiples sharing a soul and that by keeping some souls from returning to God, they could prevent the rapture—until the appointed time. An Order of enlightened multiples was ordained in 532 AD." Mike's face brightened. "You know, the river Reprobus carried the Christ child across wasn't really a river."

"What was it?" I asked.

He thought for a moment. "The impossible. Reprobus couldn't cross the river alone. He'd get washed downstream. Only after he accepted his calling and the weight of others was he able to cross. That's what you're asked to do."

"The impossible? *That's all.*"

Mike bit his lip and nodded. "Do you know why Jesus appeared as a child at the water's edge?"

"I don't." I hadn't felt this open since I was a kid listening to my father tell stories.

"Because it would have been impossible for a child to cross. God's always on the edge of the impossible." Mike fished for something under his seat. "They've been right about everything so far. You eventually knew where to go."

I heard the click of the hammer and saw the shock on the stickman's face as Mike swung the revolver round and fired. White blood canon-blasted, sprayed us, and the back window. The oily fluid smelled like rotten hamburger. The stickman's torso teetered and collapsed onto the seat.

I sensed a thousand creatures on sidewalks and in alleyways watched the car accelerate.

"Damn it," I screamed, wiping the blood from my face.

"New Jersey?" Mike asked with a smug tone.

I slumped in the seat as we sailed by creatures curling their deformed snouts and licking their mangled rows of teeth.

"I saw my sisters only occasionally once we were at the monastery," said Mike, skidding around a corner. "Everything was training."

"Maybe we should slow down," I said.

"They told me my calling was to help the Witnesses."

"Who's that?"

"I hope to God that's you. I want to see my sisters again. I've spent the last seventeen years of my life waiting for this to happen. They told me to get a job at Franklin, and then one day, there you were, one of the possible chosen. There were lots of others. We couldn't be sure."

"I always thought religion was bullshit," I said, thinking about my broken family life.

"Yeah, I gave up hope after I met you. No offense, but you don't believe in anything, do you?"

I stared out the window at the mutant creatures lining up to attack our car. "I'm beginning to."

Mike laughed. "Then I realized, who we think we are doesn't matter. Our identities are nothing more than quarks within possibilities and energy. The clay jars of our bodies are confiners, segregating versions of our selves, distancing us from eternity. The greatest sin is to believe in only the representation we've built to show the world who we are. The doctor, lawyer, law-abider, dissident, mother, father, spouse, traitor, hero, and *Advertising Specialist*—they're all mere concepts that fabricate reality."

"I don't understand a word you just said."

Mike smiled. "We had to memorize that. I added the part about the Advertising Specialist."

He handed me the revolver and snapped open the ashtray. It brimmed with bullets. "Load it."

"I don't know about prophecy or *Witnesses*, but it's pretty obvious we're going to die."

Mike looked down at the gun I was aiming at him.

"Sorry." I pointed it away. "Do you think there's any way out of this?"

"In the end, two prophets will preach and the world will hate them, just as they hated the one who sent them. They will be slain in the street, and the world will rejoice and refuse them burial. After three days, the Lord will breathe life into them and they will rise from the dead."

"One of those goddamn pigs already stabbed me." I lifted my shirt and showed him my wound. "What happens if we die now?"

Mike looked but said nothing. He veered around wrecked cars on the interstate. The world coming to chaos was stunning: fires, broken storefront windows, security alarms sounding.

"That's a sacrificial wound," Mike said. "You returned to your purgatory."

"I didn't go to purgatory. I went to 42nd Street and Lexington Avenue."

"Your whole life's been a purgatory."

My insides sank into oblivion, and emotional waves crashed upon me: my apartment, cat, the AA meetings, the countless jobs and parties and party friends, my parents growing old, wading deeper into the tragedy I brought upon us all. I reasoned, but reason did little to still the pounding surf and riptide of truth. I remembered my father's cancer, my mother giving herself to death soon after. Somehow, with all of them gone, the life preserver of a lie I'd clung to my entire life, that the trigger was pulled by some foolish child, someone my family barely knew, was torn from my hands. I wept over the fact that my life had been less real than the tragedy that'd shaped it.

"How far are we?" I asked.

"Three hours."

"Do you think Andrew's there?"

"I hope so. The prophecy says twins. I don't know if any of the other candidates are still alive. Hell, I may be the only Helper left."

"What about your sisters?"

Mike stared blankly at the road. "They died on missions."

"Sorry. . . Where are they now?"

"No one knows. They ran out of possibilities." Mike wiped his misty eyes and gave a halfhearted chuckle. "Mastema controls heaven now. I don't know what happens if we die.

"All I know is multiples must follow their hearts to the place their soul was born, and God will enter the world through his Witnesses."

"And you think that's me, an alcoholic from New Jersey?"

Mike shrugged. "I hope so."

"So, why didn't Mastema kill us when he had the chance?"

"I don't know. Maybe to follow us? Maybe he thought we'd actually round up humans for him. I'm pretty sure if he knew we were multiples he would have killed us. I don't think he knows only multiples are unchanged."

"I think he knows," I said. "I can feel it."

God cannot live, I know, one moment without me,
As soon as my life ends, He, too, must cease to be.

—Angelus Silesius

~ FIFTEEN ~

ANDREW X

For three days and nights explosions shake the city, leveling New York, knocking buildings into piles of steel bars and rubble. I wait, clinging to the promise of my new life and seething over what's been taken from me.

I long to be with Reliance again. She's been lost since I shook hands with Mastema.

The sounds of war finally cease and the city is a wasteland. Only three buildings stand in a triangle. The civilized world I knew intuitively from James's experiences lies pulverized.

Mastema retrieves me from the spot I found to watch and think. He wears black leather with etched-in-bone woven around the peaks of his muscular chest and arms. A black and maroon cape flaps behind him—a flag declaring regal power. His face is hard-lined and emotionless.

I follow him through hallways lit with emergency lighting. It's like tracking the clergy through the monastery, only now I have a leader who won't vanish suddenly and expect impossible bravery. There's nothing to fear.

We ascend in an elevator with two pigmen. They ride along like docile pit bulls.

The doors open and Mastema commands the pigs to guard its entrance. He leads me through a plush, top floor suite and onto a balcony.

The chants of a riotous mob sound from the ground floor, a mile below the slick walls of polished glass and steel. Mastema takes in the monstrous crowd and raises his arms, as I'd seen him do at the smoldering farmhouse. The horde cheers and clacks with an unimaginable roar. They engulf the ground like warring insects.

"Children! The old God is dead!" Mastema declares to the gruesome animals.

The creatures raise their barks, yelps, and snorts to the overcast sky. The stickmen's clacks deafen.

Mastema's voice booms. "A new era has dawned. You are the future. Go forth and multiply. Bring me the humans! Bring me the souls!"

Mastema points to where Reliance hangs, suspended in a cage between the three buildings hundreds of feet off the ground.

The crowd cheers.

I curse, thunderstruck, and lean over the balcony railing. "What is this? What are you doing?"

Mastema steps back inside, his cape drags like a reptilian tail, and I follow, pleading, "Please, let her go!"

"The old God is not yet dead," Mastema admits. "He's hiding. A coward tucked away in some crevice of the universe. But, he will soon have no one to believe in him, and he will die like his creation."

I gather my courage. "What are you doing with Reliance? Why did you cage her?"

"It's not your concern what I do. You pledged her to me."

"I did not!"

Mastema's voice rattles the windows. "Silence! You belong to me. All of you. Did you not think this included your soul?"

"My soul?" My knees weaken near collapse at the revelation. Until now, I'd been blind to what having a soul really meant.

Mastema laughs and lies back on a couch, a prideful sneer crossing his face. "You humans think so highly of yourselves, yet you don't know your own souls! Who did you think she was?"

I clamber to the window and peer at Reliance swaying hapless in the bitter, mile-high wind. I thought back to my prison, and when I knew her as the woman in white on the edge of the forest.

Tears well. "I didn't know."

Mastema sits up. "Forget about her. Grand things await you, far greater than the likes of that whore." He motions me closer.

I hesitate, fearing the cool, black slant of his eyes, his inhumanly large build. "Come here," he growls, and I snap to attention.

"Do you want to know the secret of creation?" he asks.

I pause, speechless.

His tone breaches giddy. "Faith in the triune concept." He pauses for recognition.

I shake my head in ignorance and disbelief.

His laugh smells of charcoal. He taps his long narrow finger against his skull. "There's personal reality, the physical reality we share, and a third reality: the reality of creation."

"Oh," I say, without understanding.

"Are you wondering why I'm keeping you alive?" he asks.

I stay silent.

He towers over me. "God is nothing but faith in a dream. Man gave God his skin of self, identity, a structure for existence, a temple of preconceived ideas. That's why God *cares* for the legitimization of self. Belief is nature's greatest commodity. Whosoever has the lion's share is The Creator." He looks past the balcony to the swaying cage and his fractured prisoner, her body vulnerable to every element in the world.

I try to silence the pangs of responsibility in my heart.

"From this seed," he says, "I will create a new heaven and earth. All men will know I am god."

"What seed?"

He points. "From that bitch out there. The cries of souls are nothing but the meaningless drone of children to the ears of the old God. I will be different and all will obey."

I sink deeper into the suede leather and agonize, knowing there's no answer for the evil I face, and no way to trek the path I've chosen.

Mastema gapes at the cage. "Soon she will birth the first of my children. Then, I will be the creator."

For every choice we make, a numberless multitude of options are left untried.

— Reverend Mother Raymunda Adair

~ SIXTEEN ~

JAMES VIII

Mike and I drove slowly at night, trying to go unnoticed. We spent the days in vacated homes, sorting through people's belongings; scavengers, longing for a sense of place and reality, something to tie ourselves to the way things were before everything changed.

Everyone has drawers and closets where they hide things, treasured objects linked to memories and their souls, experiences that formed who they once thought they were, before they devolved: Photo albums, forgotten cats and dogs, children's goldfish. I viewed the pictures, fed and released the pets, and made believe for a content moment that these people were me, that the lives they'd carved out for themselves fit into who I was today.

We lounged in a living room, watching recorded cartoons and tried to forget the beasts that threatened our lives and identities. The stench of their territorial spray lingered near the boundaries of our consciousness. I checked the serene neighborhood outside the window for any signs of them and sent up a prayer for my cat, Crank, who I hoped was alive.

A block away stood my childhood home, suffocated by thriving vegetation. I couldn't bear to stay there.

I'd kept the place for years, despite the well-paid-for pleas of psychiatrists and twelve-step leaders. The house ended up being a place of empty sobs and emotional dry heaves, a place my heart wept throughout my life—in between binges. I wondered if Andrew could really be alive, if I could connect with him again, and make amends somehow for the life I'd taken.

Now in a borrowed home a block away, we waited for the hammer to fall, for my misguided agreement with evil to run its course.

The salty grease of microwave popcorn and the cartoon's antics provided little comfort. I turned down the volume while the Roadrunner beeped on the TV. "It's been three days and no one's showed. Do you think they'll come for us?"

Mike leafed through a photo album. "They'll find us."

Hours ticked by and nothing happened—no flood of mutant creatures, no earth-tearing tornadoes from the sky.

I stayed awake most of the night and woke to the smell of coffee, burnt toast, and pleasant morning light streaming through the drapes.

My spit tasted acidic. "Please God tell me it was all a bad dream."

"You awake?" Mike asked from the kitchen.

I wondered and tried to wrap my head around the world changed forever, never to be the same.

The bookshelves were stacked with children's videos, sports trophies, and framed pictures of a family I'd never met, happy and squinting in a midday sun. They all resonated fear, the reactor core glow from a bomb you regretted making.

Mike yelled from the other room. "I found some eggs."

I sat up and rubbed my neck. "Why the hell did we drive all the way to New Jersey? Could I have been wrong about where we needed to go?"

Mike didn't answer.

I walked to a bookcase, took a volume, and turned to the first page of Dante's *Divine Comedy*.

Midway upon the journey of our life

I found myself within a forest dark,

For the straightforward pathway had been lost.

Dante Alighieri, *The Divine Comedy*, Inferno I, 1308

Further in I read:

And lo! towards us coming in a boat

An old man, hoary with the hair of eld,

Crying: Woe unto you, ye souls depraved!

Hope nevermore to look upon the heavens;

I come to lead you to the other shore,

To the eternal shades in heat and frost.

Dante Alighieri, *The Divine Comedy*, Inferno III, 1308

And even further, I read:

"My son" the courteous Master said to me,

All those who perish in the wrath of God

Here meet together out of every land;

And ready are they to pass o'er the river,

Because celestial Justice spurs them on,

So that their fear is turned into desire.

This way there never passes a good soul;

And hence if Charon doth complain of thee,

Well mayst thou know now what his speech imports."

Dante Alighieri, *The Divine Comedy*, Inferno III, 1308

These passages spoke to me as though alive. They made sense though I didn't fully understand them. I walked to the kitchen in a daze.

Mike set a plate of scrambled eggs and charred toast in front of me. "Breakfast."

I thanked him, ate, and read the passages aloud. "I learned about this in college, Charon ferrying the dead across the River Styx. He's the Grim Reaper."

Mike read the title. "Did you feel drawn to it?"

"I don't know. I just picked it up and turned to the part about the river."

Mike shoveled eggs into his mouth. "It could mean something. The Order aren't the only ones who traveled to other worlds."

I held the book tightly. "I wish it meant something. We need a clue about now."

"One of the things we learned in the monastery," Mike said, "the thing they really stressed was how everything is tied together: religion, myth, the sciences, the subatomic world, the psyche, and spirituality. They all add up to one incredibly simple yet profound equation. Maybe your picking up that book wasn't chance?"

"You mean like fate?"

"Yeah."

"I don't believe there's a force controlling what we do," I said, though I wished I could blame my decisions on something other than me.

Mike crunched into an apple. "Not controlling, directing. You have a choice. You said it yourself; you'd like that book to mean something."

I took a deep breath, trying to clear the fog from my head. "It's probably just my mind trying to find meaning where there isn't any."

"Why would you say that?"

"Because that's the way the mind works. It looks for meaning and patterns where there aren't any."

"But you did find meaning."

"Maybe. But how do I know if it's real?"

Mike smirked. "It's all *real*."

He followed me into the living room.

I looked out the front windows at the cookie-cutter houses beyond. "That makes no sense. I always imagined I'd settle down in a place like this when I found the right woman."

"Need creates reality."

I rapped my knuckles on the coffee table. "I'm talking about *real* reality."

"Reality's reality. Our need for meaning creates the conditions for meaning to exist."

I stared at Sanders, the big-boned, red-headed man who used to work in sales. It occurred to me there was a lot I didn't know and many worlds left to explore. "Are you saying we create reality?"

Mike rubbed his chin. "We create what we need."

"So, we created God?"

"No. If man created God, man would be God, and our psyches couldn't handle it. Trust me, many have tried. God made us so we need him. That's how The Creator exists."

I fought for comprehension and surveyed the media on the coffee table, magazine covers splayed with trendy celebrity photos. An old newspaper headline read: "Children Abducted from New Jersey Neighborhood."

"Why is everyone turning into animals?" I asked.

"They're not *turning* into animals. They already were animals. The veil's off, that's all. The pig is the pig, the wolf is the wolf." Mike set his plate on a picture of Tom Cruise and Katie Holmes. "Thousands of years ago, people knew that more than one world existed, they just didn't have a name for it. Then along came Quantum Physics 'proving' other worlds exist. Science claimed the discovery, but the concept existed thousands of years before. So you tell me, what makes reality the concept or the discovery?"

I shrugged. "No idea."

"The *concept* is the most powerful thing in the universe."

"More powerful than God?"

"It's all the same. Once a concept is born, it's out of the womb forever. Your problem is you've been taught that if it isn't categorized by science it isn't real."

After recent events, I didn't claim to know what was real. "Do you think we're going to survive this?"

"Good, evil, love, hate, most of reality is made of concepts, even the world we used to live in."

I scanned the electronics, furniture, and knickknacks that engulfed us. "Most people I knew were concerned with 'stuff.'"

"Yes, but each of those things was a concept before it was created. This neighborhood was imagined before it was built."

I nodded, though I doubted.

"We learned most of this by visiting the worlds on Saint Christopher's map," Mike said. "I think the map was God's way of giving us a glimpse of the true structure of things— *God's concepts.*"

"Why would He even care whether we knew about that?"

"Because, we have roles to play in His creation, just like Saint Christopher did." Mike's eyes glazed with thought, and he grew quiet, then he slapped his leg. "Of course, without the Witnesses there would be no observer, no collapse of the probability wave into a single state of reality. That makes perfect sense."

"What?"

"Mastema is evil and evil wants what it's always wanted: to reshape itself into everything that God is, because of envy. The only way to do that is perception, making one reality out of all possibilities. Mastema needs the Witnesses. He needs your belief. That's why he kept us alive."

I shoved the books aside. "I don't get it."

"If Mastema is viewed as God by everyone on earth, Mastema becomes the creator. Evil is viewed as good and everything will be thrown into chaos."

I spoke slowly to make sure I understood. "So, don't view Mastema as God?"

"Right, make sure you believe in God, not Mastema."

I hadn't believed in God since I was a child, now all of reality depended on it.

Mike looked concerned.

A silver tour bus drove past the house, gleaming in the midmorning sun. We ran to the curtains and watched it hiss to a stop, a block from the home of my youth. My heart leapt when Andrew got off, but then he got off again and again, until there was group of nine or ten that looked like him—like me.

Mike and I sprinted outside to the place where my brother's possibilities gathered. One with a scarred face introduced himself as Carter.

A woman who looked like Renee stepped off the bus wearing a somber smile. Her right arm was bundled in a makeshift sling.

She embraced me with her free arm. "James? I'd given up hope you were alive. Good job, Michael."

Mike joined in the hug, and tears flooded my eyes.

The woman looked softer than Renee and had no tattoo of a man jumping into the valley of her breasts.

She took my hand in hers. "I'm Charlotte. You knew one of my possibilities."

I squeezed her hand in recognition. "I did."

Her expression turned smug. "Not too well I hope. I was on assignment, so I sent Renee to help. I came as soon as I heard about the attack on the monastery and met up with these possibilities near the fighting." She stopped and looked around. "Where's Andrew?"

"I was hoping you'd found him," said Mike.

Charlotte pressed her face against Mike's chest. "I prayed both twins would be here. I fear it may be too late."

There was a moment of silence while we observed the sidewalk and lawn, the house of my childhood hidden behind overgrown bushes and trees.

"Never felt right selling it," I said, somewhat ashamed of its neglect.

Each of the war-torn lookalikes, the remnants of my brother's possibilities gathered around us. They wore fearless yet heartbroken expressions.

"We fought like soldiers," Carter said, "taking out twice as many of them as they did us, but there were too many."

Charlotte shook her head. "It's hard to believe. The place of sacred liminality is a rundown house in New Jersey?"

Mike wiped tears from his eyes. "We don't know that for sure."

"It'd better be," Charlotte said. "Time's up."

Mike took in the house. "Sometimes the sacred is not what it seems."

Carter leaned against the idling bus and covered his wounded face in his hands.

"You led well," said Charlotte, patting his shoulder. "There was no more you could have done."

Carter didn't respond.

I was proud that Andrew held the possibility of Carter.

Charlotte looked me in the eyes. "We barely escaped with our lives. Some of your brother's possibilities fled the battle."

I didn't know what to say.

"Everyone has those possibilities," said Mike.

"They left us for dead," Charlotte said. "We barely made it to the bus in time. They gave over the remaining souls for execution. I hate to say it, but I think we need to deal with the possibility that Andrew has sided with Mastema."

I wanted to say it was impossible for Andrew to act so cowardly, but somewhere inside I sensed it was true. I suddenly understood the expressions on the lookalikes faces. They were children who'd learned their father had committed the most heinous of crimes.

Carter pushed away from the bus and faced the lookalikes. "We're our own people. Remember that."

They looked disheartened.

"How much of a person can we be without a soul?" Someone muttered.

"You're all good," Charlotte said. "Look at yourselves. You're on the side of The Creator."

Shamed for Andrew, I couldn't say a word.

"I'd rather live as a good possibility than a human who uses free will for evil," voiced Carter.

"But we can't change, we can't grow," said another.

"Can Andrew come back?" I asked. "I mean, if he's gone over to Mastema's side."

"You made an agreement with evil," said Mike.

"So what," I said. "I take it back. I didn't mean it."

"What did you agree to?" asked Charlotte.

"To turn over the remaining possibilities and souls in exchange for a guilt-free life," said Mike.

Charlotte scowled. "You'd do that?"

"Of course not. I was just buying time."

"I doubt there are any other humans left out there anyway," Charlotte said. "The three of us may contain all the remaining possibilities."

"And Andrew," Carter said. "Time will tell whether or not he will believe in Mastema as god."

"I won't," I said, confident in my unbelief.

Everyone was quiet. I sat before the fence and walkway to my parents' home, the one I'd unknowingly reserved for this moment, and dreaded my thoughts. I questioned the addictive bits and pieces that made me up and wondered if my resolve would stand the test of fire. I remembered hiding near the edge of the river in Zenith, running from an unnamed fear.

Charlotte stood nearby on the sidewalk and addressed the group. "Just as the prophecies say, God has been cut off from the world. We must assume Andrew's joined Mastema!"

Panic spread throughout the group.

Carter joined us on the sidewalk. "If James and Andrew are the Witnesses, we must protect their soul, Reliance from Mastema."

"They're the only ones who can bring God back into the world," said Charlotte.

Mike grabbed my arm. "They're right."

"I've got nothing to lose," I said. "The world I knew is gone."

"That's the spirit," said Carter, perking up.

"Only one thing," Mike said, "where are they?"

My heart weighed heavy in my chest. "That's the only thing?"

Everyone looked past the fence and the overgrown bushes to my parents' dilapidated house.

"Perhaps the answer's in there," said Charlotte.

"He's already been inside when we first arrived," said Mike.

"Try again," said Carter.

"What's going on?" I asked.

"You can tune into each other," Mike said, "even right now."

"Because you share the same soul," said Charlotte.

"But in a place of liminality," Mike said, "where your soul was born, you can see even farther."

Charlotte shrugged. "Maybe before wasn't the right time."

Mike grimaced at the house with its peeling white stained paint. "Is it dangerous? I mean, if Andrew has joined with evil?"

"I don't know," admitted Charlotte.

"What other choice do we have?" asked Carter.

"None," said Charlotte.

Mike sat beside me. "Are you up for this?"

Suddenly, I longed to be back at my Advertising Specialist job and for things to be the way they were. When Mike was simply a nuisance I could ignore, and my fights were against a familiar enemy. Everything I'd ever struggled against was now coming after me, and none of my old tricks worked.

"I don't understand," I said. "It's just a house."

"Hopefully, it's much more than a house," Mike said. "It's a place between worlds."

"Be careful," advised Charlotte.

"Of what?" I asked.

"Careful of believing that Mastema is god," said Mike.

"Careful of joining him more than you already have," said Carter.

I stood in a huff. "Why on earth would I join him?"

"Why would Adam and Eve eat of the fruit?" asked Charlotte.

If there was one thing I'd learned from all my years of addiction recovery it was who I could trust. And right now, I was the only safe bet going.

The house beckoned. I pressed my hands against my legs to stop them from shaking, suddenly thirsty for a Captain and Coke.

The years following Andrew's death surfaced: watching my parents age, leaving their home to claim my own life—one I never believed I deserved.

I questioned the other's belief in my destiny. Saving myself seemed as unattainable as saving the world and neither appeared worth the effort. But, there was only one path before me.

I walked to the door, turned the handle, and eased it open. The dim living room was filled with yesterday's new things, covered with dust cloths. Behind me, beyond the overgrown shrubs, Mike, Charlotte, Carter, and many possibilities silently cheered me on.

I stepped inside and closed the door. Unlike before, memories leapt from the corners of the room. Running feet smacked against the upstairs floorboards. I turned, reached for the door handle, and then hesitated. Someone giggled. I turned back and faced a Christmas tree, shining with the brilliance of a perfect moment. My mouth dropped. Gold, red, blue, and green lights winked on and off, ornaments gleamed, a white-winged angel adorned its summit.

A cry sounded upstairs. The tree burst into flames that licked at the ceiling. I scaled the staircase two steps at a time and stumbled into my room. It looked as it did in my youth—two single beds, plaid sheets, toys, and sports gear.

A shot rang. I turned, stunned at the sight of my parents' open bedroom door and the darkness beyond.

My stomach tightened into a ball. I took deliberate steps toward their bedroom. Around the corner of their bed, I saw my brother's little white sneakers, his ankles, legs, and then all of him, as I'd seen him the day he died. I hid my face and agonized at the sight of his head hanging by bloody fibers.

I ran from the room. Vast air swirled and cage bars surrounded me. A horrendous mile-long drop loomed below.

A beautiful woman lay naked, curled in a fetal position on the cage floor. I knelt by her side and reached out, but my hands passed right through her, as though I were a ghost. She looked up at me and blinked away the sun.

"Can you see me?" I whispered, noticing the stretch marks on her plump stomach.

She looked to one of the three towering buildings supporting the cage that held us. Andrew stood on a balcony, staring blankly. He turned and walked inside.

"Can you see me?" I repeated.

She gave a faint nod.

"I'm going to save you." I said.

She cried out in pain.

I tried reaching for her, but my hand passed through her again.

Lime-green liquid exploded from her womb, and I woke, prostrate on the dusty bedroom floor. Everything was as old as it should be; restored to the past I'd left so many years ago.

I got to my feet and looked out the curtains at the silver bus and the lookalikes breaking into one of the nearby homes.

The horrors I'd seen flashed, holiday lights in my mind. I ran downstairs and slammed the front door behind me. Mike, Charlotte and the others gathered around.

"What did you see?" asked Carter.

In tears I shared my vision, including the destroyed city, the three skyscrapers, and the caged woman.

"The triune concept," said Charlotte. "I'm sorry; the woman was most likely your soul."

"My soul?" The blood rushed from my face. My legs felt weak. "But how can that be?"

Mike put his hand on my shoulder. "It's what we were afraid of. . . . What did the buildings look like?"

I hesitated, overwhelmed by what I was hearing. "Like skyscrapers. I think I saw the Bryant Park fountain."

Mike looked shocked. "Right near where we used to work?"

"It couldn't be New York," I said. "Oh, my God. They destroyed New York?"

I felt a flame spark inside and slowly take me over. I'd longed my entire life to know I had a soul, and now that I did, I'd do anything to save her.

"Evil's destroyed far more than a city," Carter said. "We must fight to restore God into the world."

"There are too many," said Mike.

Charlotte surveyed the neighborhood and the hazy-blue sky. "I agree. We can't defeat them with force."

Carter looked at Mike, Charlotte, and me. "We may still have an army. You all have possibilities left."

"I don't have the possibilities I once had," said Mike.

"Nor do I," said Charlotte.

"So what then?" asked Carter.

"The Witnesses must lead," said Charlotte, looking at me.

"That's what the prophecy says," said Mike.

"Only they will know how to bring God back into the world," said Charlotte.

"But, I don't," I said. "I have no idea how to do that."

Charlotte and Mike lowered their heads.

I stood tall. "I will do anything to save my soul though."

"What about the book you found this morning?" asked Mike. "You said you needed it to mean something."

"Yes," I said, "but what?"

Mike sighed. "That's up to you. You're the Witness."

"We still don't know that," I said.

"There's no one left," screamed Carter. "I wish I could do it!"

I tried to remember the passages I'd read. "Maybe there's another book, or something else. Something's missing. I don't think I'm who you think I am."

"The map." Charlotte checked her satchel with her uninjured hand, pulled out Saint Christopher's map, and unfolded it. "Dear God." She held the map out for everyone to see. "It's changed. There are only two worlds."

"What does that mean?" I asked.

"I've never seen this before," said Charlotte, her voice trembling.

Mike took the map and examined it. "It means whatever Mastema's doing, it's affecting reality."

Carter leaned in. "Has he destroyed the other worlds somehow?"

"I think he's creating new worlds," said Mike.

"They can't possibly last," Charlotte said. "Everything will collapse in on itself. Lord in heaven, Mastema must be making new souls and merging them with those monsters. It's the only way for him to create something otherworldly."

"How can he make new souls?" I asked.

Mike and the others averted their eyes and didn't answer.

Charlotte took the map back. "We're running out of time."

In the very earliest time, when both people and animals lived on earth, a person could become an animal if he wanted to and an animal could become a human being. Sometimes they were people and sometimes animals and there was no difference. All spoke the same language. That was the time when words were like magic. The human mind had mysterious powers. A word spoken by chance might have strange consequences. It would suddenly come alive and what people wanted to happen could happen—all you had to do was say it. Nobody could explain this: that's the way it was.

—Edward Field, *Magic Words*, 1998
Translated from the oral tradition of the Inuit

~ SEVENTEEN ~

ANDREW XI

Reliance sways night and day in her cage as her belly grows large. The monsters send her food and water using ropes and buckets. She eats and drinks barely enough to keep herself alive.

From the suite where I watch the world change, I call to her when the guards are distracted. She doesn't answer. She screeches terribly from birth pains.

From the balcony I cry, "It must be this way, but only for now!" I have no idea how to save her.

An evil horde gathers on the ground far below, horrible ants seeking bones to crunch in their jaws.

Reliance wails, and phosphorescent green liquid spills from her suspended cage. Her pleas reach the vacant heavens.

Mastema bursts through the suite's double doors, his cape and pigmen guards trail behind. He wrings his hands and meets me on the balcony.

Reliance bellows in agony.

Mastema chuckles. "It's started."

His voice booms over the pigs, wolves, stickmen, and the landscape of ruble below. "This is the first of many souls, my children, the true souls of your father."

The crowd gives a hellish cheer.

Mastema nods to his pigmen guards, and they heave on lines fastened to the cage with deformed hoof-like hands, inching it closer.

Reliance is barely recognizable, skin and bones except for her rounded stomach. Her eyes, once fresh with life seem unnaturally dark. She peers at me through the blond locks of her mangled hair.

Across the suite, the elevator dings. Three stickmen burst out and clatter to Mastema's side. They meet the cage as it swings onto the balcony. A pigman opens the cage door. Reliance lies inside, straining, trying to catch her breath. A forest of blood-red scratches cover her pale body.

I watch, helpless, as the stickmen clack into place for the birthing. I fight back tears. She screams and a bloody head emerges from between her legs.

The stickmen pulls out the child, snips the cord, and places the infant in Mastema's waiting arms. He sneers, walks to the edge of the balcony, and holds out the infant to the mob below. The creatures' outpour rattles the earth.

The infant girl grows with the speed of spirits, reaching the size of a four-year-old in a matter of minutes.

I kneel beside Reliance and cradle her head in my hands. She turns away.

The new soul learns to walk. She stumbles to a table lined with glazed turkey, chicken, bread, cream, assorted grapes, pears, peaches, and many other foods. She eats as though starving and reaches adulthood in no time—a monstrous beauty.

"Take your residence," Mastema says, motioning to a wolfman, who pants excitedly in the open elevator.

The new soul patters toward him and the door closes behind her, concealing a brilliant flash of light.

Reliance looks up at me, fatigued and shivering. I cover her with her dress and whisper, "I'm sorry."

"Get away from my bitch," screams Mastema.

The stickmen nudges me back. I hold fast to Reliance's arm. A stickman strikes my chest, knocking my breath out.

"Prepare her," says Mastema.

The pigmen lift Reliance, naked.

"Where are you taking her?" I scream.

"To the breeding room, so she can ready herself." Mastema turns to the pigs and rubs his groin. "I will be in shortly."

"You promised me life," I say, sickened.

Mastema looms over me, growing large in his fury. "Is it not enough for you to believe in me as your god?"

I sink low. "I believe. Please, treat her gently."

A serpent's smile slithers onto his face, and he struts to the balcony. He looks out over his followers and their vast destruction. "Don't be small-minded. The soul directs the spiritual essence of every living being. Once your twin believes in me as god, I will give you a new soul worthy of your belief. Your brother did not return to me as he pledged. I will not be so kind to him!"

I join Mastema on the balcony, a tiny flame of hope ignited within me. "James is alive? Where is he?"

"Hiding along with the God of the past. They will both be sorry."

Three tortuous days pass.

I try to dull my mind from pain, but it's impossible to block out all that surrounds me. I wonder if this feels anything like the addictive haze my brother has battled.

I watch from my balcony as the creatures below part for eleven possibilities dressed in the same T-shirt, jeans, and sneakers as me.

The travelers negotiate the jeering beasts and hike toward the towering skyscrapers at the center of the world. I greet them on the ground floor and usher them upstairs to the suite where they eat from the feast table. They share stories about running from Carter's battle.

I know the damnation in their eyes and hear it in their accounts of fleeing at the expense of their brethren. They're old friends guided by thirst, hunger, and desperation. The return of these possibilities gives me hope of claiming my new life.

The birthing process takes less time than before. The phosphorescent green liquid pours more freely, and Reliance's flesh-peeling screams come less frequent.

A wolf enters the suite and awaits a newborn soul, arriving as the others had, on the elevator one by one. He hunches on two legs near the elevator. His snout quivers as he sniffs the air. His winter-night eyes watch as his soul is born.

The child toddles to the feast table, devours milk and food, and walks gleefully into the wolf, uniting in a brilliant flash. A moment later, the wolf is like a man, standing upright and proud. Only something isn't right. His features are grim like Mastema's, his skin unnaturally pale and smooth, as though stretched to breaking. Something eternal lives in him, but I sense it is a rocky wasteland. I hate what he is.

Mastema clasps his hands with achievement and gives a narrow-eyed smile, as he does each time a soul and creature are united. "After this life," he says, "you will exist forever."

"I believe I will," says the man-creature, accepting his benediction. He kneels, takes Mastema's hand, and kisses it. "Thank you, my god and creator."

I'm as amazed now as the first time I witnessed this.

"Where did the child go?" asks one of my lookalikes.

"They're one," I say, horrified.

"But where did the child go?" asks another.

I answer as Mastema answered me, "A new world."

Mastema peers down at me as a stern father to a child, and I realize my essence is growing. I feel strong in my anger, as if I need no one.

A stickman clacks beside me, its pencil-thin hands luminous green from the womb of my soul. I grab an iron lamp and swing it with all the rage in me. I strike its head, a mace to a melon. Its body cracks to the floor.

Mastema laughs from his bronze-hard belly. The lookalikes slowly back from the creature's hissing remains.

"Why did you do that?" someone asks.

I don't know. "Because I can."

Mastema gives a lone clap of approval.

"You're a monster," says a lookalike with a red-raw wound across his face.

I approach him with the lamp, and the others around him cower.

"Are you going to strike yourself?" he asks.

I hold up the lamp. "If need be."

His indignant fawn eyes stare back.

My arms fall to my sides. "Carter?"

He punches me. I land on the floor, blood filling my mouth. The lookalikes spread about the room, pulling handguns from under the legs of their jeans.

They fire.

White blood splatters.

A pigman raises his arms and squeals.

Mastema grows larger than life, swinging his arms side to side, knocking lookalikes about the room like toy soldiers. They line up and fire at him, but the bullets have little effect. The room darkens. Mastema rams into a bunch of lookalikes, grabbing their heads and knocking them together. He swishes his arm through empty air and sends three or four flying into walls. The new man-creature lies on the floor. A crimson pool oozes from two gunshot holes in his torso.

A blood-splotched pigman pins Carter to the ground and chomps at his neck with jagged teeth.

One of the lookalikes kneels beside Reliance. He's different from the rest with a stitched cheek.

I call out, "James!"

He motions for me to join them, but I'm afraid to move—torn between fear-filled hate and a glimmer of mercy. I take a step, but stop.

Still air blooms into wind, swirling about the room and cage. James and Reliance whisper a chant over and over. Mastema smacks the heads of two more lookalikes together. They crumple to the ground beside him. He gallops toward Reliance and James, as the current of air increases. My brother and soul vanish in a flash, leaving Mastema reaching for nothing. He fills the suite with a dark lion's roar and scans the bodies strewn about the room with blazing eyes.

All things transitory

But as symbols are sent.

Earth's insufficiency

Here grows to event.

The indescribable

Here it is done.

The Woman Soul leads us upward and on!

—Johann Wolfgang von Goethe, *Faust*, 1808

I am not a mechanism, an assembly of various sections.

And it is not because the mechanism is working wrongly, that I am ill. I am ill because of wounds to the soul, to the deep emotional self—and the wounds to the soul take a long, long time, only time can help and patience, and a certain difficult repentance long difficult repentance, realization of life's mistake, and the freeing oneself from the endless repetition of the mistake which mankind at large has chosen to sanctify.

—D.H. Lawrence, *The Complete Poems*, 1977

~ EIGHTEEN ~

JAMES IX

I carried the battered woman on my shoulders, in a new world marred by evil, a place of rocky desolation. We descended a path on the side of a pitted mountain, overlooking an expanse of cliffs and crags.

In the distance, in one direction, a sizzling, red desert stretched to the horizon. In another direction, the landscape was matted with snow and ice. And in between, where we were, a leviathan-sized storm brewed, drawing the planets and stars into milky blackness. Claps of thunder sparked wicked bolts of lightning, striking nearby mountaintops.

Her voice was raspy-angelic and close to my ear. "Where are we?"

I scanned the rock face for the others. "The other world."

I knew Andrew's soulless possibilities, the lookalikes in the suite, couldn't follow us into this new heaven. For them, pretending to be their less honorable counterparts in order to rescue this woman, and possibly Andrew, had been a suicide mission. I knew this but didn't fully realize it until I saw them destroyed and found myself here alone with who they claimed was my soul. I whispered a prayer of thanks.

I stumbled on loose shale and hurried down the mountain path, holding her body wrapped in a tattered white dress. I was glad Mike and Charlotte were still out there, somewhere. They'd told me to find a safe place to hide, because Mastema would follow. They'd told me whatever creatures with souls died in the other world would arrive here in their afterlife.

I remembered the *new man* I'd seen killed and scanned the crevices in the surrounding rocks, unsure of what hideous form he'd taken here.

Drops of rain tapped on the stones around us, appearing in an instant and increasing to a hazy deluge. I rushed ahead and ducked into the entrance of a cave, nothing more than a crack in the rock. The air inside was still and frozen. I laid her on a bed of gravel and looked out at the gray curtain of rain spraying in near the cave's mouth.

It was difficult to believe I'd stolen back my soul. She looked sick, thin in places and bloated in others.

Behind her a passage led into pitch blackness. The cave could be only several feet deep or might go on for miles into the heart of the mountain. I had no way of knowing how to keep us safe.

"Are you all right?" I asked.

She didn't answer.

"What's your name?"

Her weary voice carried a hopeful tone. "Reliance."

"You're my soul?"

Her chapped lips turned up. "I am. You knew me when you were a boy."

I wondered how I could I have forgotten such beauty, but I knew somehow it had to do with what I believed I deserved.

Outside, in the splattering rain, a towering figure dressed in black robes trod past the entrance, followed by a lesser figure in plain clothes hiding his eyes from the downpour. The man stopped, and I sank farther back.

He looked straight at me. It was Andrew, his eyes piercing the haze and blinking away the rain.

Mastema returned and followed Andrew's gaze to where we hid. Andrew tried to look away, but it was too late.

Mastema sauntered to the cave's entrance. Andrew moved in front, gesturing as though he'd seen us farther down the path, tugging on Mastema's cloak. Mastema slapped him to the ground and peered in, his immense body blocking the light, shielding us from view. He sniffed the air like a hunting dog and tried to enter, waving one arm through the cracked entrance and forcing the rocks apart with his chest.

He sang a wretched song. "Come back to me, my sweet. We have new worlds to make."

Reliance curled into a ball.

He dislodged himself, lifted Andrew by the neck, and thrust him into the cave. Andrew crawled out of Mastema's reach and held the side of his face. We stayed quiet and slid farther in.

Mastema's voice shook the mountain. "I am god! You cannot run from me!"

Rocks and silt fell. I trembled and reached for the comfort of Reliance's bare skin, imagining her unharmed and complete in the dark.

Andrew crawled next to us. My trust was tested.

"Bring them out," barked Mastema.

I tried to see though the blackness. "Let's go."

"Bring them out," Mastema demanded again.

"Go to him," Andrew pleaded. "He'll bring the entire mountain down on us!"

For a moment I listened in fear, the part of me that clung to the bottle all my life. I'd always run from reality, but this time it was to save my soul.

I kneaded Reliance's scrawny arm to still my shaking hands. "We have to go deeper." I lifted her onto my back and crawled farther into the cave on all fours. Her feet dragged behind. Her arms held me weakly.

Mastema's voice thundered over the raging storm. "Come out now!"

My knees bruised on the stone ground. I called to Andrew and heard no reply. I reached into my pocket, pulled out my cell phone, and flipped it open. The light showed the cave grew larger farther in. A dark form moved close behind us. I pointed the light toward it.

Andrew blinked and shielded his bruised face. "He'll kill the new creatures and send them in here after us."

Mastema roared outside and tried to edge his massive body through the cave's entrance.

I stood and helped Reliance put on the dress I'd taken off the cage floor. I lifted her onto my shoulders and tried not to think of what nightmares might live here.

"He needs you alive," Reliance said. "He needs you to believe in him."

We pressed on, navigating sharp-edged rocks until we could no longer hear the sky's rumbling, and the sliver of light from the cave's entrance was lost.

A few squares of cardboard lay beside my foot. I motioned for Andrew to hold the cell phone. "What are those?"

He kneeled and brushed topsoil off a baseball card. "Mickey Mantle. We had these when we were kids."

I stared in awe at the cards littering the ground. "What is this place?"

Andrew quickly shuffled away, leaving us in the dark. "Look at this."

I stumbled toward him and saw scattered Christmas tree ornaments, some broken, some intact, some half-buried in stone, reflecting gold, silver, and ruby-red egg-like shells. There were also plastic Santas, miniature metal trains, drums, and two Huffy bikes embedded in the rock.

"Do you know what this is?" I asked, Reliance.

Her eyes barely opened. "Pieces of you," she said. "Evil made this world with what's inside you."

We crept through the dark until the cell phone light dimmed and with it any hope of finding our way. Reliance eventually gained the strength to limp along with us.

For an eternity, no one said anything, until I gathered the courage to voice my heart. "I'm sorry, Andrew."

He said nothing.

We heard only the shuffle of our steps.

I reached out and found the arch of Reliance's back. "How could you do this to her?" My words echoed through the cavern. "Answer me!"

"I never meant to hurt her," replied Andrew.

"But you did."

"You took my life," he said, "before I had a chance to live."

I bowed my head. "I know. I'm so very sorry. Were you trying to hurt me through hurting her? She doesn't belong to us. You let her be raped!"

"I'm sorry," said Andrew. "I only wanted a life of my own—like you had."

"You think I lived! How could I live when every day of my goddamn life I thought about the brother I killed? I didn't mean to kill you. You're alive now!"

"In this place," Andrew said. "It's too late!"

"Now's the time for both of you to live." Her words were a breath of air to drowning men.

A deranged growl echoed from somewhere far off in the cave.

"They're coming." Andrew quickened his pace.

We rushed through the darkness, frantic, cutting and bruising ourselves, trying to stay together and get away.

Hellish shrieks closed in.

I clasped Reliance's hand in mine and tried to help her along.

"We're lost," Andrew said. "We should have gone back!"

I feared he was right, but moved as quickly as I could, waving my hand in front and feeling ahead with the side of my leg.

The sound of clicking insects surrounded us, as though we were food in a hive.

Holding tight to Reliance, I called out to God. "Please! Whoever or whatever you are. Help us!"

The clicking sounds intensified, until it felt as though hideous bugs burrowed in my ears. I let go of Reliance and tried to brush them away, curling into a ball on the ground.

"Where are you?" I cried, seeing only an empty void around me.

After the longest time, amid the crawling darkness, I felt hands searching for my arms and helping me to my feet. Only then did I see the far-off pinprick of light—a sun burning a light-year away. "Do you see that?"

"Yes," answered the others.

We limped toward the hopeful speck, trying to catch our breath. Our path grew lighter while hell rushed at our heels.

Near the exit, I saw how bruised and bloody we were. Shrieking demons advanced in the obscurity behind us. They were semitransparent, bending light to shadow, horned and both flying and gripping the rocks above and below with talons.

We ran into the blinding light outside and sprinted down a barren hillside, toward a river that sliced through the mountainous landscape. The air moved behind us with the beat of wings. A demon swooped down, as I dove and tackled Reliance flat upon the ground. The winged beast soared past, its claws snapping open and shut. In the light of day, these beasts had the heads of men and birds, and the bodies of mangled angels, clear as gelatin, exposing their veins and organs. Their legs were bent and their feet pointed with fierce claws. They twisted and deformed the chalky sky when they moved, swooping down one after another.

"The river!" I screamed.

A demon latched onto Andrew and picked him up with a great beating of wings. Andrew squealed like a snared rabbit and struggled his way free, tumbling head over heels onto the ground.

Another tried for Reliance. I jumped and shoved the demon as it flew low. Its talons slashed my ribs. A blood-red streak rose in the air above us.

We helped Andrew to his feet and ran together under a sky morphed by transparent devils.

Down the hill, a small wooden boat rested on the shoreline. A hunched figure wearing a black hooded cloak stood onboard. His face and hands were hidden, and a long pole leaned on his shoulder, extending into the frothy, midnight-blue river.

Andrew climbed aboard. "It's the only way across."

I tried to hold him back. "That's not the way."

The figure came alive suddenly, bringing his pole out of the water and pushing it down to cast off.

"Come on!" Andrew sat down. "He's here to take people across."

The boat slid swiftly into the water. I ran and held fast to the end of it, sinking past my knees.

"Climb on," screamed Andrew.

My eyes opened wide. Behind Andrew, the land on the other side of the river dripped with lava and fire. A million lost souls writhed in flames. The figures cloak flapped in the wind revealing the spiny bones of a skeleton. "Charon!"

The pole struck my head.

When I came to, Andrew was beside me in the water, looking shaken. The ferryboat battled the current to the far shore with Charon alone. The landscape beyond was now the expanse of rocky fields and mountains we'd seen before.

I turned to the sound of screeches. Reliance stood on shore holding a young boy's hand. Behind her, Mastema left the cave we'd escaped, his arms raised to the chalk-gray sky. He was larger than ever and charged the river under the swarm of circling devils.

Reliance and the boy met us in the water. There was no time to ask questions. The child reached up with open arms, and I lifted him onto my shoulder. Reliance took my hand, and we pushed deeper into the water.

"Andrew, come on," I shouted.

He hesitated, then caught up and grabbed Reliance's hand.

The water coursed, walling against us, trying to drag us to the depths. Our feet slipped on riverbed stones.

I tried to brace the mysterious child on my shoulder. He seemed to grow heavier with each step. He clung to my shoulder and neck as I swallowed water.

My feet lifted from where I'd set them, and I flew backward from the current's unbelievable force. At first Reliance held me, then she was caught up, swinging with

Andrew onto the other side of me. My hand tightened around hers, crawling toward her wrist for a better hold.

Andrew lost his grip and tried to fight the current on his own. He leaned in and grasped for Reliance's outstretched hand.

The demons slashed, razors from the sky, skimming the water and lashing at us, tearing away chunks of our flesh, and screeching in glee.

Andrew touched Reliance's hand but couldn't lock fingers.

I tried to inch closer, but the child weighed on me, and I choked on water. I nearly let the child go, but my conscience clung even tighter.

Andrew searched my eyes as he charged against the current. "I forgive you, James."

In an instant, he was caught by the force of the river, tumbling, reaching up, trying to breathe—and drowning.

"No!" My heart tumbled after him, ripped from my emotional insides. I shed agonizing tears and watched helplessly as he struggled and gave up, disappearing under the surface.

It took a moment for the finality to sink in. There was no other world for him to go to. His body was dead and his soul with me.

We trudged across, one step at a time, dodging the attacks from the sky, our flesh torn and bleeding. We staggered onto the other bank. I lowered the child to his feet. Reliance and I leaned on each other and collapsed onto dry ground.

The demons landed and surrounded us. They lurched forward, mechanical dolls with deathly life breathed into them.

Mastema crossed the river in a matter of strides and stood over us, gargantuan and seething. "Declare I am god, and I will spare your lives!"

He looked ready to crush us with his bare hands.

I looked up and lost my breath. Tears clouded the most beautiful sight I'd ever seen. The child was Andrew, the way I remembered him. I hadn't realized before.

He gave a fine, youthful smile, and the fear of losing him again locked onto me like the teeth of a rabid dog.

I forced myself to stand and saw my height was barely to Mastema's waist. I faced him, standing in front of Reliance and young Andrew.

Mastema laughed from the pit of his belly.

"Unus mundus" . . . *the multiplicity of the empirical world rests on an underlying unity, and that not two or more fundamentally different worlds exist side-by-side or are mingled with one another.*

—C. G. Jung

Whoever finds his life will lose it, and whoever loses his life for my sake will find it.

—*The New International Version Bible*, Matthew 10:39

~ NINETEEN ~

ANDREW XII

I know who I am in an instant, birthed from forgiveness. All of my selves and their possibilities unite without regret, freeing my heart in triumph.

Beside me, Reliance, the essential soul of the universe lies battered. She's not important because she's mine. She doesn't belong to anyone. Her importance is because in the darkest moment of her existence she clung to the knowledge that regardless of the dreams of man or evil, she would never die.

With us now, among the gruesome horde of demons, is God. Not as I imagined before, but as God truly is, the binding force that is in all things, the force that causes the baby bird to fly or fall from its parent's nest, and the force that rotates the heavens on a course that seems their own.

James stands between us and evil, dwarfed by Mastema. And I am reborn, a child again. Demons writhe in anticipation. They reach toward us with veiny, see-through arms.

I pray. The wish is within me, hanging in the essence of this place and everywhere, instantaneously, as though I'm in all things and all things are in me. In a moment, Mastema appears small and the demons pitiful.

Mastema lunges at James, trying to pick him up. My brother smacks away his hand. He tries again. James lands a fist to Mastema's face, knocking him backward onto the ground.

The demons recoil in fear.

Mastema stands and rubs his jaw. He raises his arms to conjure destructive power. But, the skies don't move. Not one of his followers flinch a transparent muscle.

Behind us, the horizon awakens, as I imagine it. A searing light decimates all shadow in its path, sweeping across the rocky cliffs and valleys.

The demons retreat in horror. They fly with great speed toward the cave, but the light encompasses the entire world in an instant. Mastema and the demons fall and explode. Their insides splatter with puffs of smoke.

We endure, unfazed by the light's intensity. Calmness and daylight cleanse the landscape.

I understand why Saint Christopher never argued with destiny, why he stood as a guardian for good, never bending under the immense weight of embracing something larger than himself. He understood his actions were a part of something so profound as to be everything, even God. And in this, we imagine The Creator that already exists, and He imagines us. The knowledge of all I previously learned amounts to nothing.

I see both far away and very close: Charlotte and Mike Sanders in a fantastic meadow of another world, lying with each other under the shade of a tree, there to rebuild and be parents of all women and men on a very old and new earth.

The creatures, great and small, regress to animals of the field, fleeing the sight of man and existing as they are now meant to.

As for us, over time, the grass begins to grow. At first, in between the razor-sharp rocks, and then, over eons, on top, covering any trace of the thorny dimensions of this place. As the children on the mortal plane grow old and die, they visit James, Reliance, and me, and help us make a new heaven from a place that started as hell.

ABOUT THE AUTHOR

After a near death experience, author Christopher Hawke realigned his life with what matters most. He started EcoSpiritLife.com, a website supporting spiritual and nature-oriented retreats and classes. Currently, Hawke works as an intuitive Life Guide, a spiritually grounded mentor dedicated to helping others align their lives with passion and possibilities.

His debut novel, *Unnatural Truth*—a surreal psychological thriller focusing on the perception of reality, addiction, and mental illness established Hawke's unique talent for storytelling. His prose weaves together philosophy, spirituality, psychology, and terror into deep stories for deep people.

For more information about Christopher Hawke and his work explore the following resources:

EcoSpiritLife.com

ChristopherHawke.com

UnnaturalTruth.com

AlteredSelves.com

We hope you've enjoyed reading *Altered Selves*...

Printed in Great Britain
by Amazon